THE REDEMPTION

By David Boiani

Foundations Book Publishing Company
Brandon, MS 39047
www.foundationsbooks.net

The Redemption
By: David Boiani

Cover by: Dawné Dominique
Edited and formatted by: Steve Soderquist
Copyright 2019© David Boiani

Published in the United States of America
Worldwide Electronic & Digital Rights
Worldwide English Language Print Rights

ISBN: 978-1-64583-042-9

Dedication

For my grandparents, who, regretfully, were not alive to read any of my literary works. I hope, for selfish as well as altruistic reasons, they are able to read them in spirit.

Dedication

For my grandparents, who, regretfully, were not alive to read any of my literary works. I hope, for selfish as well as altruistic reasons, they are able to read them in spirit.

Table of Contents

Acknowledgments

Writing fiction has become my salvation and I truly wouldn't be who I am today without it. I would like to thank all the authors who have inspired me throughout my life to take this journey. Thanks to Leah for your artistic talent and my editor, Steve Soderquist. Thanks to my mother and father. Thanks to Ro for your help and support. Thanks to Laura Ranger who helped me create a kick-ass website. Thanks to all my beta readers. Thanks to my bandmates, Artie, Matt, and Sean for being my inspiration behind the three clowns at the bar. Thanks to Amy for your support. I would also like to thank Brenda, my beautiful daughter Gianna, and everyone who reads *The Redemption.*
I hope you enjoy reading it as much as I enjoyed writing it.

CHAPTER ONE

Nathan Jefferies opened his eyes. As his vision sharpened, the world slowly but steadily came into focus. What Nathan saw caused him to yearn for the oblivion of unconsciousness to return. Above him was a large glass vat with a spout on one end, containing a clear liquid with a yellowish tint. He noticed a faint scent of sewage; panic came over him as he thought: *sulfuric acid.* A chain was attached to a crank and secured to the side of the vat opposite the spout. Nathan tried to sit up but he was restrained by chains, one secured to each limb. He quickly looked around and saw he was lying in what resembled a glass coffin. The room was small, with one door and one window. Nighttime shadows came through the window and played on the far wall. There was one, faint light bulb hanging from the ceiling, dimly lighting the room.

How did I get here? Nathan thought.

His eyes returned to the acid in the vat. He heard a *click* as one link of the chain cranked up, and the liquid inched toward the spout. *Holy shit, it's timed!* he thought. Nathan flailed his arms and legs, trying to free himself from his restraints but to no avail. He was tightly secured.

"Help!" Nathan yelled with all he had. Nothing. After a few more futile attempts, he stopped.

As his coherency returned, he tried to remember anything he could. He recalled his morning jog while absorbing the sun's early rays. His run was interrupted as he approached a black SUV that was pulled over due to a flat tire; he had stopped to help the motorist mount the spare. The last thing in his memory was turning to look at the tire, and then he woke up here.

Another *click* from above and the liquid inched closer to the spout. Nathan thought of his family: his wife, Andrea and his two sons, Zachary and William. He yearned to see them again. How could it end like this? Nathan always wondered what it would be like to live inside a horror movie; to feel the adrenaline and panic of knowing your life hangs in the balance, living with the uncertainty of your outcome and how much pain you would endure. Nathan glanced at the window and noticed the first sign of morning as the room started to brighten a bit, with the virgin sunlight of a new day.

Click.

The fluid was at the end of the spout now. One more link and it would drip onto him. The spout was aligned with his face, a mere three feet above him. He noticed something in the far corner uncovered by the morning sunlight; a video camera pointed at him with an illuminated green light. Someone was recording this.

"*Stop this, help me, please!*" he screamed at the camera.

Click.

The first drop fell onto his right eyeball. Nathan's sight turned black as he screamed in pain.

Click.

Click.

Click.

John Corbin sat at his desk, crunching the previous day's sales numbers as a prideful joy came over him. The Sufficient Grounds Tavern had been open three years and it was an overwhelming success. His partner, Red, had introduced John to a wonderful chef, Pete Darby, whom Red had prior connections, both being in the restaurant business. John had a good feeling about Pete and thought his culinary talents were a perfect fit for the menu John had imagined. The Seattle Cuisine, a local dining and entertainment magazine, had done an article on the Tavern and gave it a spectacular review. People started to flock in, sampling the cuisine and enjoying the nightly entertainment. Red not only managed the bar, he also waited on customers to help out the staff.

John placed the computer printout into the safe and locked it just as Red knocked on his office door.

"John, Captain Johnson is here to speak with you."

"Thanks, Red. Send him in."

"Sure thing."

John's thoughts flashed back almost four years ago to the day he confessed his sins to the captain in the interrogation room. The captain was due to retire at the end of the year, and John was planning on throwing a huge bash for him at the restaurant.

"Hi, John," Captain Johnson said as he walked into the office. The two comrades shook hands and the captain sat down across from John. "How's it going?"

"Perfect, couldn't be better. The restaurant's thriving, I'm married to a woman I love and respect, and my children are happy and healthy. What more could I want?"

"Glad to hear it." Captain Johnson smiled. "Is the restaurant business everything you thought it would be?"

"It's challenging, but I like the test. I like to compete. There will always be people who are more intelligent, more talented, and more gifted, but I can outwork them — that's the one quality I can control."

"That's a great attitude. If only more of the population felt that way," Captain Johnson said.

"Give me the rules with a level playing field, and I'll compete with anyone. That's all we as citizens can ask. So, how are you doing, captain?"

"Lately, not so well, I'm sorry to say."

"What is it, trouble at home?"

"No, my home life is fine, however, the station is a different story."

"Go on."

"We have a new psychotic malefactor on our hands, but not serial yet. He's killed two, but it's only a matter of time until he strikes again."

"What makes you so sure?" John asked.

The captain pulled out his cell phone and brought up a video.

"Watch this."

John took the phone and watched as the screen came to life. The video showed a man shackled and chained inside a glass box. As the man awakened, he immediately struggled to free himself but failed. He stopped his struggle and looked around the room, noticing the camera and pleading to be set free, moments before a liquid substance drips onto his face from above. Seconds later, another drip falls, followed by another. Before long, the man's face is gone, replaced by a mask of melted flesh. John places the phone down in disgust and leans back in his chair.

"John, the un-sub sent a live feed to my station email. We watched the scene play out, in real time. We were helpless. I don't need to ask you if you realize how frustrating that is for us."

"Were you able to trace the email address?"

"I put the best IT experts on it and they told me the un-sub went to extensive lengths to secure the email account and video feed, so no. He or she anonymized the IP address and encrypted the feed, whatever that means. My people couldn't break it."

"So, you have no idea who the perp is, or why he's doing this."

"No, that's why I came here, John. I need your help. You're the best. I know more are coming, and he won't stop until we find him. I need to nail this scumbag to keep people safe so I can retire with a clear head. I know this is a tough spot for you, and I wouldn't ask if it wasn't of the utmost importance to me. This one makes me feel like I'm the target of some sick, twisted universal joke, like the whole world is laughing at me. It's disturbing."

John nodded in sympathy. "Captain, you know how much I respect you, also, you know you're like family to me, but I've ended that part of my life. It took some time and some soul searching, but I've made that transition. I'm a restaurant owner now. I can't go back." John searched Captain Johnson's eyes and noticed the desperation and the weariness.

"John, there's something else you need to know."

"Go on," John replied as he sat back in his chair with his hands behind his head.

"At the end of the video feed, after the victim had passed, there was text on the bottom of the screen." The captain paused and let out a deep sigh and looked his friend in the eyes. "He asked for you, John."

"Me? Why?"

"We don't know. He just typed your name with an ellipsis following. 'John Corbin...'"

John dropped his head and looked down at his desk with thoughts racing through his mind. "Give me a day to think about it."

"Of course, take as much time as you need."

Captain Johnson got up, shook hands with John and walked out, leaving him alone to ponder his decision. As John glanced around his office, he gazed at the picture of his wife, Julie, and their children, Gianna and Ryann. He thought about the possible consequences his decision may have on them. He then saw the picture of his former partner and friend, Todd McGrath and his wife, Jacqueline, on the night they were enjoying a dinner together. On that unforgettable evening that now seemed like a lifetime ago, Todd had informed them of Jackie's pregnancy and their plans to marry. Months later, John had found them strangled to death in their home, left on the dining room floor by their killer, a man named Silas Alvah. That was the last case John worked on.

Now that he was finally content in his new life, could he possibly get pulled back into that one? Innocent lives were at stake, and that had always been his primary concern. John headed home to sleep on his decision, his mind a whirlwind of thoughts and emotions.

Even with minimal sleep, John was up early the next morning. Julie had left for her shift at the hospital, leaving him alone to toss and turn over his decision. Once he decided what he wanted, he would be better prepared to discuss it with her.

John headed to the bathroom to shower and shave. When finished, he made breakfast for his children, Gianna and Ryann. As he placed the eggs and toast on the table, he looked and noticed Gianna, punctual as usual.

"Good morning," John said as he glanced at her. Now thirteen, John at times saw the woman that his daughter would soon become, although still having the look of an adolescent at other times. It was confusing to John, so he could imagine how confusing it must be for her. His daughter was growing up and that reality bothered him for no matter what age, we always see our sons and daughters as young children, innocent and pure.

"Hi Daddy," Gianna said.

"Can you wake your brother and bring him down for breakfast? Use force if need be," John said with a smirk. His daughter smiled back.

"Sure Daddy."

John dropped the children off at school and returned home to walk Simba. The Alaskan Malamute was now three-years-old and weighed close to ninety pounds. He clipped the rope lead onto Simba's collar and headed out the door. John paused for a moment to feel the warmth of the sun's rays. It was a beautiful May morning.

Simba waited patiently as John finally looked down. "Let's go, boy." Simba reacted with a quick trot toward the street with his long tongue hanging happily from his mouth.

After the walk John headed to the restaurant. The fresh air and the scent of the hemlock and pine trees cleared his mind and now he needed to make a decision. It was Red's day to open and John wanted to hear his opinion. He pulled his truck into his usual spot, walked in, and sat at the end of the bar.

"Hey, John," Red said as he walked up to greet him. "Did you forget it was my day to open?"

John shook his head. "Hi, Red. No, I need to talk to you about something." John looked toward the other end of the bar. "Red, who the heck is that?"

"That's Sean."

"Sean?"

"Yeah, he's always here. I let him in early when I open. He was waiting in his car when I pulled up."

"I thought he looked familiar. Doesn't he work?"

"Sure, he's a driver for one of those new transportation network companies. Kind of like a private taxi."

"Does he know it's 10:00 a.m.?" John added as he glanced at Sean, which brought a quick wave from his patron.

"I don't think that time comes between Sean and his beer," Red answered with a chuckle. "What did you want to talk about?" Red took a seat next to John.

"When Captain Johnson visited yesterday, he informed me of a new killer on the loose. He's murdered two already, and all signs point to him continuing his run."

"Okay, so what is so special about this one?"

"He sent a feed via email to the station containing a video of the victim being executed."

"Why?" Red asked.

"I assume it was just to toy with them. My guess is he wants to display the control he has over the force. He wants to make them feel powerless and useless, suffering through the experience of knowing innocents are being murdered, let alone watching it actually happen."

"So, the captain wants your help with the case?"

"Yes, that's part of the reason. I'd like your opinion."

Red didn't hesitate. "Don't worry about this place. I have your back. I can handle it on my own if you want to take a leave."

"Thank you. Aside from this restaurant, what are your thoughts?"

"You're a detective. It's in your blood and your soul. If you feel that itch, it must be scratched."

John sighed. "I've worked so hard to turn the page on that part of my life, I'm not sure going backward is good for me. If I open it again, will I be able to close that door a second time? I feel like Michael Corleone. 'Just when I thought I was out, they pull me back in.'"

"You ever see a housecat hunt mice or birds? They're generally well-fed, and don't do it for survival. They follow their instincts. You need to follow yours. Killers will kill, and you catch them. That instinct will never go away. It's embedded in your soul. John, you were never out... you were on leave. It's what you were born to do. I say go for it. It's your decision, and surely you need to talk to Julie, but know I support any decision that you make."

"Thank you, Red." John glanced around the restaurant, admiring what he and Red had spent the last three years building. He glanced at Sean, who looked back and raised his beer in a salute.

"But John, you said helping the captain was only part of the reason. What's the other part?" Red asked.

John looked back at Red and let out a long, slow sigh. "The killer asked for me personally."

Red gave an understanding bow of his head, patted John on the shoulder, and said, "Take as long as you need."

On the ride home, John contemplated how he would broach the subject of continuing his detective career to Julie. They had finally put John's life on the force behind them, along with his questionable decisions and activities that led to his retirement. He was certain Julie wouldn't be as supportive as Red had been, but he needed to try to explain it all to her. He had to make her understand why he needed to do this.

John flipped on the radio and scanned the stations as he pulled his truck onto the highway. A song that fit his current mood, Bon Jovi's *Dead or Alive*, bellowed from the speakers as John sat back to listen. Though not the band's biggest hit, John thought it was their best work. He continued down the highway as he took in the song's old west guitar riff, imagining walking into the station with a cowboy hat on, carrying dual colt revolvers in western gun holsters like the old-time cowboys. When the song came to an end, the disc jockey thanked the listeners for supporting Seattle's home of the oldies.

"What? What the ...? When the hell did that happen? That's not an oldie," he said out loud while glancing at the radio, as if the jockey would apologize for the station's mistake. Though flustered and insulted by the station's obvious error, John saved Seattle's home of the oldies to his #6 preset-button. John gazed at his reflection in the mirror with a cluster of thoughts racing through his head. He knew in his heart the decision was made as soon as Captain Johnson asked him for his help. John yearned to feel the tension, anticipation, and thrill of the chase leading up to the elation, gratification, and pride of the capture. He knew being a detective made him feel alive, and the truth was, he felt a rush flow through his body that had been missing the last three years. The only problem was informing Julie. He flipped off the bathroom light and crawled into bed beside his wife.

"Baby, we need to talk."

"Is everything all right?" Julie asked as she quickly sat up.

"Yes, it's just... something came up."

"What is it?" Julie asked. John saw the look in her eyes before the sentence was out of her mouth. That look told him she already knew.

"John, no. You can't."

"Listen, Julie, it's only one case. The captain needs my help. I owe him my life, and my freedom."

"How do you know, John? How do you know the same result won't come of it? How do you know the same feelings won't surface, your need to protect and bring justice? What if your need to institute revenge for the victims returns? How do you know it won't all come crashing back?"

"I honestly don't know, but I am different now. Even if those feelings and thoughts resurface, I can control them now."

"How do you know that, John? This isn't a game. This is your life, our lives, our children's lives."

John noticed the distress in his wife's voice. He couldn't stand the thought of hurting her, or the children.

"Listen, I'll go see Dr. Grant and get his professional opinion. If he thinks it's a bad idea, I won't do it."

"But why, John? Can't you just let it go and move on?"

"Julie, we can't change who or what we are. I was born a detective, and I'll always be a detective. That's who you married. I need to do this."

"Why is this case so important?"

John held her face in his hands and looked in her eyes.

"The killer asked for me."

She gasped as a tear ran down her cheek. "Why? Who is he?"

"I don't know, but I need to find out. I'll go see Dr. Grant." John held his wife to his chest and kissed the top of her head.

John glanced around the reception room as he waited for the doctor to call on him. He glimpsed quickly at two fellow patients, a man maybe ten or twelve years older than John and a younger woman who looked to be in her thirties. His eyes locked with the woman's and she immediately looked down. Over the last three years, John had perceived the anxiety that is present in a psychiatrist's waiting room. It's as if everyone was determining your level of crazy when they looked at you. John pondered what her story was and whether Doctor Grant's therapy was helping her. He looked away quickly, not wanting her to notice his interest in her mental state.

"Mr. Corbin, Doctor Grant will see you now. Go right in," the receptionist said with a smile.

"Thank you," John replied as he headed for the doctor's office.

Martin Grant greeted John as he entered. "John, how are you? It's been awhile."

"Hello, Doctor Grant, I've been well, thank you," John said as the two men shook hands and sat down, John on the couch, and the doctor on his oversized armchair.

"So, what brings you in? Are you having issues?"

"On the contrary, I've been doing very well. I've settled into my current life as a civilian, restaurant owner, father, and husband."

"That's fabulous. What can I help you with then?"

"I need your professional opinion."

"Go on," Doctor Grant replied.

"I'm considering going back into the field," John paused to look at Doctor Grant's reaction, but saw only a stoic, empty face. "Just for one case, then I'll go back to my current life. I would like your blessing; not only for me, but also to ease Julie's concerns."

Doctor Grant's eyes stayed on John as he took in his patient's disclosure. "John, I saw something in your eyes as you declared your desire to go back to detective work. What I saw, was desperate and pleading. You may not even realize it, but you have no intention of working just one case. Are you still having nightmares?"

"Yes."

"How often?"

"Weekly," John replied.

"Okay, lay down on the couch. We're going back to the night you killed Silas Alvah."

John stared at the ceiling, his head resting on a pillow and his hands folded, relaxed, placed on his chest.

"Now, close your eyes and relax. I want you to go back to that night, the night you strangled Silas Alvah. Imagine you're there, reliving it now. How do you feel as you walk into his lab?"

John's mind thought back...

It was Friday, 5:45 p.m. John pulled up to the lab, parked his truck, and walked in. The lab closed at 6:00 p.m. so John knew his interrogation of Mr. Alvah would not be disturbed.

"I feel excited, intense, angry."

"Okay, now you're walking up to the desk to speak to him for the first time. Do your feelings change?"

John remembered...

He walked up to the front desk and waited. Mr. Alvah soon appeared. "Hello, Detective Smith. How are you? What can I do for you?"

"No, I want to prove his guilt to myself, so I can take his life and avenge the death of my friends."

"Now your hands are on his throat. Do you feel any hesitation? Do you feel any remorse as he slips away?"

The fog lifted, and this violent memory slowly came into focus...

With a scream, John put his hands around Silas' throat and squeezed as hard as he could. A faint, angelic smile played over Silas' lips and his eyes were at peace. They no longer contained anger or hatred. Silas had accepted his fate, and he welcomed it.

"No. I feel vengeful, exhilarated. I feel whole again."

"Silas Alvah is dead on the floor underneath you. Do you have any regrets?"

John's memory fully returned...

As John continued to squeeze, he saw Silas' lips mouth, "Thank you," as his eyes closed and he drifted away, free from Earth; free to finally meet his Maker. John let go of his throat, got up, took one last glance at what he did, then walked out.

"No."

"Would you do it all again, John?" the doctor softly asked as John's eyes shot open and he briskly sat up, placing his hands over his face.

"John, you're not ready. Your PTSD is still very much a factor. You have what we call, delayed-onset PTSD. You have made progress, but in my professional opinion, you're not ready to resume detective work. It's too risky."

John stood and walked to the door. He turned and said, "Thank you, doctor, for your opinion." He then walked out of the office. John would never see Doctor Grant again.

***

Later that evening John sat at the kitchen table nursing a scotch, dreading what he was about to do. Through everything, John's honesty was always present, and now he planned to mislead his wife. He glanced at the clock while taking his last sip of scotch. It was five minutes to midnight and the house was quiet. He rinsed the glass, placed it in the dishwasher, and headed up the stairs to their bedroom. He paused at the door as he felt his stomach churn, closed his eyes, and took a deep breath before entering. Julie lay in bed reading a book. John undressed and crawled in next to his wife.

"What are you reading?"

"Dark Musings, It's a collection of shorts stories. It's a very intense read."

"Is it horror?" John asked.

"No, not really. It's more a psychological thriller, but it can be frighteningly real at times. I find that even more disturbing than straight horror."

"Interesting," John said.

"What is it, John? I can see something in your eyes."

"Am I that transparent?"

"To me you are."

"I'm sorry," John replied.

"Don't be, honey. I like that I can read you so well. I know most can't, so it makes me feel special. Now, what is it?"

"Doctor Grant is on board with me returning to my work."

Julie paused and put her book down. "John, your work is being a restaurant owner."

"I'm still a detective at heart. He thinks I've progressed to the point that my issues are behind me." John noticed a look of concern and pain overcome Julie's face. "John, this scares me. Do you know how long it took for me to accept what you did? If I go through that again, I'm not sure we can recover."

John took Julie's face gently in his hands. "Trust me, baby, I'll be fine. *We'll* be fine."

"But what if we aren't? What if you lose control again?"

"A wise man once told me his definition of hell: on your last day on earth, the person you are will meet the person you would have been without fear holding you back. I don't want any more regrets. I still have work to do. That chapter of my life isn't closed. I can't accept that. I need to do this."

Julie dropped her head and remained quiet for a few minutes, which seemed an eternity to John.

She finally said, "Okay, baby. I believe in you."

John smiled and held his wife tightly.

"Thank you, my love."

"So tell me something. Who was this wise man?"

"Um, well, he was a drunk in a bar."

When their laughter died down, John made love to his wife deep into the night.

CHAPTER TWO

A chill went down Kerry Reid's spine as she waited on the side of the dark, winding deserted road. Fifteen minutes had passed since her white Optima stalled, and she called for roadside assistance. She had dialed her fiancé, Steven, but there was no answer. He's probably at the gym, she thought, as she checked the time.

Headlights appeared in her rearview mirror and she felt a wave of relief, hoping that it was help arriving early. She sighed as her hopes passed as the black SUV drove by and continued down the road. Moments later, headlights approached from the opposite direction, and the same black SUV pulled up beside her. Through the darkness, Kerry could just about make out the outline of a man's face. He rolled down his window and motioned for her to do the same. She hesitated, but then followed his lead, stopping the window halfway.

"Hi, need some help?" he asked.

"It stalled and won't start. I called roadside assistance. They should be here any minute."

"Sometimes they take much longer than they say they will. You shouldn't be left out here all alone. Let me take a look."

"No, really, I don't want to be a bother. I'll be fine."

"Nonsense," he replied.

Before Kerry could respond, she watched him pull his SUV up behind her. A cluster of thoughts cluttered Kerry's mind as the man's door opened and she heard his footsteps approach her door. She turned and glanced at him for a moment, pondering her next move. The man's innocent, handsome face and his calm and friendly demeanor overpowered her survival instinct and she opened her door and stepped out.

"Pop the hood, I'll get my tools," the man said.

She reached in and grabbed the release, then walked around to the front of the car and raised the hood. As she turned back, something connected with the side of her head. She fell to the ground in a heap with an explosion of pain overtaking her. The last sight she took in was the man's black leather boots as she faded to black.

Kerry opened her eyes slowly and her vision reluctantly returned. Her arms were in restraints secured above her head. Her surroundings slowly came into focus. She was in a large open barn with lofts on both sides supporting bales of hay. The throbbing pain from the wound on her head made her wince and she could feel the dried blood that had dripped over her ear and down her neck. She struggled to regain her focus and shake the cobwebs from her mind. *Where the fuck am I?* she thought. Something came into focus twenty feet in front of her. A shotgun, perched on a makeshift platform, pointed directly at her head.

"No, please...!" she shrieked. "Somebody, please help me!"

The barn door slid open and a man entered and approached her that she recognized. It was the man in the black SUV. Kerry felt herself shake in fear.

"Please... why?"

The man's eyes looked at her for just an instant before walking to the shotgun. Kerry watched as the man seemed to be attaching something to the trigger. She flinched and tried to pull free but was unsuccessful. The restraints were secure.

"Why?" she pleaded, as tears ran down her face. He looked up one last time before walking out of the barn. Kerry looked back at the shotgun to see what he came in to do. Attached to the trigger was a latch, secured to a pulley. The pulley was connected to a small device. It read 23:58:33. The device was a timer.

"No, please! Somebody, please help me!" she screamed as her bladder let go. She felt warm wetness run down the inside of her thighs. Nobody heard her. She looked back at the timer. It read: *23:58:01, 23:58:00, 23:57:59...*

Captain Johnson sat behind his desk in his office, lost in thought, as a knock on the door snapped him back to reality. He glanced through the glass to see Ricky Burton, his new and promising – albeit young – detective who had just transferred from the East Coast. Ricky had his head bowed and his hands by his side, waiting patiently.

"Come in, Detective Burton," he said.

As Burton entered and approached his desk, the captain noticed his walk was filled with confidence, bordering on arrogance, with a glide that looked like he didn't have a care in the world.

Look at this cocky little fuck strut, he thought as a smirk played on his lips.

"You wished to speak to me, Captain?"

"Yes, Mr. Burton, have a seat. We need to go over a few basic procedures and understandings. Son, it's a pleasure having you. I'd be hard-pressed to remember an addition to my team who had the credentials, training scores, and the sparkling resume you possess. Only a year and a half in the field and already a detective! That's quite an accomplishment, and very impressive. Welcome to my force, son. I'm pleased to have you."

"Thank you, sir. I'm happy I transferred here from New York. I look forward to many years of service."

"Excellent. Having said all that, there are a few things I would like to discuss with you. Being a detective carries a bit more responsibility and attention to detail. Seattle isn't New York. You'll learn how to work with a team here. Your fellow officers are a constant source of support and aid to be valued and respected. Don't underestimate the power of chemistry in the force and the shield."

"I understand."

"I hope you do, son. You're going to be working the new case with me. There are two dead already, and we need to put a stop to this psycho. I'm sure the feds will get involved at some point, but we need to do our best to catch this asshole as soon as possible."

Captain Johnson opened a drawer on his left and handed the detective a manila envelope, thin with information. "Here, take this folder and brief yourself."

"Will do captain."

"That's all for now."

Captain Johnson watched Ricky Burton walk out of his office, hoping his speech would leave an impression on his young detective. Good, young talent was hard to find, and he hoped Ricky would blossom into a star. The truth was, Ricky Burton reminded the captain of himself when he was a young detective. He needed guidance then, just like Burton does now. His cell phone buzzed as his wife Sarah called.

"Hi, honey."

"Hi, Michael. Will you be home for dinner?"

"Yes, slow day. I could use a hot meal."

"What time can I expect you?" she asked.

"The usual time."

"Okay. See you then, sweetie."

Just as Captain Johnson turned off his cell phone an email notification came over his computer:

Just for you, Captain...

He opened the email which had a link attached. He clicked on it and a video feed came onto his screen. As his eyes took in the setting of the video, his stomach lurched. He saw a woman, secured by restraints to her wrists, attached to a beam in the rafters. She looked to be in a large, airy open building. A warehouse or a barn. Captain

Johnson felt a bit of panic overcome him when he noticed what was in front of the woman: a shotgun, set up on some sort of stand, aimed directly at her head. There was text on the screen that seemed to be counting down...

23:59:45, 23:59:44, 23:59:43...

He picked up the station phone. "Stan, we got another feed. Get the IT experts here ASAP. Also, send Burton in." He reached for his cell phone as Burton and Stan Jenkins entered his office, his wife answered on the first ring. "Cancel dinner, Sarah. I'm sorry, it's going to be a long night."

As soon as the words were out of his mouth, an additional text came over the feed. Captain Johnson put his hands on the top of his head and glanced at Ricky. Ricky looked at the screen and read:

JOHN CORBIN...

Red stood behind the bar and looked out over the restaurant as the dinner crowd started to filter in. A few regulars were present at the bar, including Sean, who waved Red over.

"Another Brooklyn?" Red asked.

"Yeah, I guess I have time for one more," Sean replied as he gave a token glance at his watch.

"You said that three beers ago," Red said as he popped the cap off a fresh bottle and placed it in front of Sean.

Matt, another regular, said," I'm sure he'll say it after that one as well."

"Hey guys," a newcomer said as he sat down between Sean and Matt.

"How's it going?" Sean asked. Red just raised his eyebrows and nodded at his new customer.

"My name is Artie," he said as he stuck out his hand toward Red. "I heard this is the place to be."

Red shook his hand. "Well now, my friend, that depends on what you're looking for." This brought a chuckle from Sean.

"Right now, I'll settle for a Blue Moon," Artie said.

"You got it, orange wedge with it?"

"Dude, you do realize that's a chick beer, right?" Matt said.

"Really? Well, I like it, especially with the added orange flavor. It's fruity."

Red smirked as he placed the beer in front of Artie.

"Do you have chicken fingers here?"

"No, sorry... here's a menu."

"Chicken fingers? What do you think, this is a fast food joint?" Sean said with another chuckle.

"Chicken fingers would hit the spot right now, especially the honey barbeque ones."

For the first time that afternoon, Sean was speechless.

Matt looked at Artie and said, "Hey. I've got a joke for you. Why did the chicken cross the road?"

"So, he could be made into chicken fingers for me. I don't know, why?"

"To get to the idiot's house. Knock, knock."

"Who's there?" Artie asked.

"The chicken," Matt said, followed with a burst of laughter.

Artie shook his head. "Alright, I walked into that one."

"I don't get it," Sean said. All three looked at each other and laughed.

Matt, after finally regaining control, looked at Artie and said, "Hey, did you know I went to Brown University? It's an Ivy League school."

"Umm, congrats," Artie said.

"Yeah, I try not to talk about it much, but it does happen to come up in conversation."

Red looked up and noticed John enter and take a seat at the end of the bar.

"Hey, what's up partner?"

"Hi, Red."

"Have you decided?"

"I have." Red noticed an uncomfortable look on his friend's face.

"What's the problem? I detect some trepidation."

"I lied to Julie. First time in my life," John said as his eyes quickly darted away.

"Ouch, well, I'm sure you had your reasons." Red noticed John's discomfort and chose to change the subject. "So, you're on the case?"

"Not yet, I will be after I talk to the captain."

"Good luck, my friend. I have a feeling you would regret it if you declined his offer."

"I may regret that I accepted it."

"True, but if you really believed that, you wouldn't have."

Red walked over to take Artie's food order as John's text tone went off.

When Red returned, John showed the text to Red:

We got another one. A woman with a shotgun pointed at her head. We have twenty-three hours.

John paused for an instant that seemed to last an eternity before typing in a reply.

Red noticed John look up as he showed him what he typed:

I'm in. On my way.

John dropped the phone in his pocket, gave a slight nod to Red and left the restaurant.

Red watched him walk out, hoping that he helped his friend make the right decision.

John drove down the highway headed to the station with an overload of thoughts and emotions running through him. The killer had asked for him personally, but why? Being dishonest to Julie troubled and unnerved him, but he was thrilled to be doing what he loved again; pursue and catch criminals. He felt an adrenaline rush take over his body as he pulled into the station parking lot and entered the building for the first time in three years.

"John! It's great to see you!" Detective Bernard said, looking up from his desk.

"Hi, Don. How have you been?" John asked as they shook hands.

"I'm great. We had another addition to the family."

"Congratulations. Boy or girl?"

"Girl, Stephanie is thrilled. She always wanted a girl, and after Jacob and Tommy, she'd given up hope. We decided to try once more. The third was the charm. Are you back with us?"

"Just for one case. Running a restaurant keeps me pretty busy. Captain Johnson asked for my help, so here I am."

Detective Bernard hooked a thumb back. "He's in his office with the new kid. John, it was good to see you again. Good luck on the case."

"Thank you," John said, then headed to the captain's office. He knocked on the door and the captain looked up from his desk and waved him in.

"John, so glad you decided to join us," the captain said.

The first time John saw Ricky Burton, he saw similarities to his younger self some twenty years ago. John noticed the chest out, the cocksure stance and the bright, intense eyes meeting his own as John walked up to the desk.

"John, this is our new recruit and your new partner, Ricky Burton."

"My pleasure, Ricky."

"Same, I've heard quite a bit about you. You're a legend in these parts," Ricky said as the pair shook hands.

"Legend may be stretching it just a bit, but thank you."

Captain Johnson turned his computer monitor so that John could view the screen. John took in the scene: a woman, hung up like Jesus himself, with a shotgun aimed at her head. On the bottom of the screen was a timer. It read: *22:34:16, 22:34:15, 22:34:14...*

"Have we identified the perps MO yet? John asked.

"No. Different gender, ages, places and times for all three victims. The only constant is the video setup and the unsub asking for you."

As John intently watched the woman on the screen, he noticed Detective Burton glance at him out of the corner of his eye. His gaze lasted a split second too long as John could feel the unease and tension emanating from the young man. This kid didn't trust him.

"Do you have any idea why the killer would be asking for you, Detective Corbin?" Ricky asked.

"None whatsoever," John said, still feeling the thick stare from across the office.

As a lone dark figure watched John Corbin enter the station, a slight smile crept across his lips. His task was complete. He had succeeded in luring Corbin in. As the dark figure leaned back in his chair, he thought: *now the real fun is about to begin.*

"Are the feds involved yet?" John asked.

"No, but I've notified them and welcomed their help now that this is a serial case," Captain Johnson replied. "So, John, what does your instinct tell you?"

"I think there's a deeper meaning here. This will escalate. I have no idea why the killer asked for me, but we need to figure that out."

"Don't give these nut-jobs too much credit. Statistics say most of them don't have a plan. They just need to quench their desires. The thought that they're analytical, calculating planners is mostly inaccurate," Ricky said.

"Maybe, but there is something going on here. The perp wanted our attention for a reason. He or she is toying with us."

After struggling with her binds for an hour, the woman on the screen seemed to relax and accept her fate.

"So, what do we have to work with here? A deserted barn, an unknown woman, and your name, John."

John asked, "Captain, do you have identification of the first two victims? How were they discovered?"

"The first victim was a homeless man in his sixties. We still have no I.D. Prints came back with no matches.

"How was he killed?"

"Suffocated. He was tied to a bed and at twenty-four hours, a gloved hand came into view and blocked his airways until he was dead. Then the video shut down. The second was Nathan Jefferies; married, father of two boys."

"He was dissolved by the sulfuric acid, correct?"

"Correct."

"Locations?" John asked.

"The first victim was found in a sleazy hotel room in Highland Park. Mr. Jefferies, or what was left of him, was located in a vacant machine shop in South Delridge."

"Victims were about an hour apart. This one must be in a rural town," Ricky said.

"We have her face. Have the feds run a search of their database for a match," John suggested.

"Already on it," the captain said, "but she would have to have a record. I think she's clean."

As the woman started to resume her struggle against her binds, new text appeared on the screen.

Welcome John, glad you could join us...

"What the...? How the hell...?" Captain Johnson picked up the station phone. "Bernard, he's watching us. I want a team to search the area, now!"

"Will do captain."

The text continued:

Now that we are all present, let's have some fun. Up for a little challenge, comrades? Or, as I like to call it, a test. A test of wills, intelligence, and persistence. John, you are known as one of the best at what you do, now I will give you a chance to prove it. This young woman's life depends on it. At twelve hours, I will send you a clue to the victim's whereabouts. You need to solve the clue and save the innocent lovely lady in the allotted time, or her life will forever be on your conscience. Good luck, and may the best prevail...

The three men looked at each other with solemn expressions. John glanced at the timer on the screen: *19:48:03...*

12:01:02, 12:01:01, 12:01:00...

John watched the time tick down towards the halfway point. He hoped the second twelve wouldn't be as frustrating as the first twelve were. He glanced through the window into the office across the hall at the federal agents huddled around their own computer.

"Their feed is working, correct?" John asked.

"Yes, they are seeing everything that we see," the captain replied.

12:00:03, 12:00:02, 12:00:01...

Suddenly, a wall of text appeared on the screen:

0469544268
9721787468
3645267078
7696343215
7447532789
6735217250
5721408867
1219219472
0712826490
0967931004

"What in fuck's name is that?" Captain Johnson said.

"There's a pattern there, hidden in the numbers. We have to figure out how and where it's embedded," Ricky said.

"How the fuck do you know that?"

"Captain, he's challenging us to find the clue. There is something here that will lead us to the victim."

"Ricky's right. What hint could possibly be hidden in a wall of numbers? Maybe a code? Each number may represent a letter?" John said.

"But there is no definitive data to use as a starting point to make the pattern decipherable," Ricky replied.

The captain turned his head sideways as he tried to make out some sense of the sequence.

"Maybe it's something famous, a poem or lyrics to a famous song," he suggested. "I'm going to run it by our friends next door. They have an expert code breaker present."

John watched the captain enter the office across the hall, then turned to Ricky. "What are you thinking?"

"I'm not sure yet. There's a program that runs algorithms on a series of text or symbols to uncover patterns. That may help us here."

"I'm talking about your gut. What does your gut tell you?"

Ricky looked at John and for the first time since they met and held his gaze.

"I don't use gut feelings when on a case. All emotion should be checked at the door, and that includes instinct. Everything in this world can be broken down into simple mathematics: numbers, percentages, and equations. It's called rational certainty"

"The problem with that theory is that we're dealing with unstable, psychotic individuals who can use instinct and emotion when deciding their next move."

"Psychopaths or sociopaths don't have emotions," Ricky countered.

"Maybe not empathy or love, but they do feel pride and have large egos, which more times than not factor into their decisions. I believe we need to combine our instincts and experience with raw data and percentages."

Ricky finally looked away and glanced at the computer screen. "On that, we can agree to disagree. But, for her sake, we better find the perfect formula to uncover her whereabouts, or we'll have another dead victim on our hands."

3:01:23, 3:01:22, 3:01:21...

John watched the time tick down as his mind tried desperately to make sense of the numbers. The feds came up with nothing. No pattern, no code, or cryptography. The frustration was building to a crescendo and the more the men pressed, the more elusive the solution seemed. The captain was next door with the feds and Ricky stepped out to get some air and clear his head. Alone, John studied the numbers. If there was no code or pattern, the sequence numbers must mean something. Maybe a zip code or an address? But with just over three hours remaining, there was no way they would figure it out in time. Plus, those clues seemed too vague to matter. This monster was evil, but he or she seemed to want to play this game fairly; a perfect battle of wits, on a level playing field. It had to be something more precise.

Captain Johnson walked back into the office.

"Anything?" John asked.

"No, nothing. Where do we go from here?"

"There's something here, we just need to spot it."

"I'm out of ideas. To add insult to injury, Bernard and his team couldn't find anything. No sign of anyone watching the station. This killer is like a shadow… always present but dancing just outside of our sights," Captain Johnson said.

John looked up as Ricky walked in with the same defeated and frustrated look on his face the captain wore.

"Any new ideas?" John asked.

"Nothing, this person is starting to piss me off."

"It's a man," John replied.

"How do you know that?"

"Mostly my gut, but I have a few reasons. The way he communicates through text is masculine. Also, he seems to handle these people easily, which means he's physically capable. A woman may have more of a struggle. But the main reason is ego; his desire to compete and prove how smart he is. He feels the need to prove he has superior intellect over us. Women are far less likely to care about that stuff."

"I knew a few women that care plenty about that stuff. I swear they lived to prove me wrong," Ricky said.

John and the captain both looked at Ricky and they all had a short laugh together.

***

00:38:13, 00:38:12, 00:38:11...

John's thoughts raced through his head, sweat beaded on his brow and he could feel his heart rate racing. He glanced at the innocent woman on the screen who had abandoned her struggle long ago, and now hung limply from the shackles around her wrists. She had her eyes closed. She didn't want to watch her life ticking away. John once again studied the grid of numbers. Suddenly a thought came to his mind.

"Captain, what are the coordinates for Seattle?"

"The coordinates? You mean longitude and latitude?"

"Yes."

Quickly, Ricky jumped to his feet and studied the grid with John. "Latitude is 47, longitude is 122."

"Ricky, look for a sequence of 46-48 vertically and 121-123 horizontally."

"I'm on it."

John noticed the captain move closer to the screen to join in the search. "There. 121921947 starts on the eighth row down, left to right.

"Yes, I see it. Ricky, jot the sequence down. Eight numbers deep," John said.

"Done, I see two vertically. 47732789 in the seventh row, and 47664772 in the second row, starting at the top"

"I'm getting the feds to locate those two points," Captain Johnson said as he rushed to the office next door.

"Get ready to fly, Detective Burton," John said as he looked at his younger accomplice.

"I'm always ready. Can I trust you to drive, or are you too old?"

Captain Johnson burst into the office, "Men, we have the two locations. One is Snoqualmie Trail, Issaquah. The other is Carnation Farm Road in Carnation."

"I know them. Both are approximately thirty minutes out. I'll take Ricky and head to Carnation. Send the exact coordinates to my GPS."

"I will have the locals check out each location if they can beat us there. I'll send the Feds to Issaquah."

Before John hurried out he glanced at the screen and set the stopwatch on his wrist to match the time on the screen: *00:23:58, 00:23:57, 00:23:56...*

00:16:49, 00:16:48, 00:16:47...

John drove southeast on I-5 with his siren on and police lights flashing. He knew the time was very tight, and every second mattered. He increased his speed and caught a glimpse of Ricky holding on for dear life in the passenger seat.

"Don't worry, rookie, I've been doing this a long time."

He slowed down to take exit 168B onto WA-520.

00:09:10, 00:09:09, 00:09:08...

Captain Johnson's voice came over the radio: "John, the coordinates in Carnation are on NE Carnation Road, a few miles up on the left. There's an old vacant barn that used to be part of the Talbot farm before the bank foreclosed on the property."

"Got it. I know where it is."

John increased his speed as he traveled down WA-202. He weaved in and out of vehicles and drove on the other side of the road when he needed to. He turned left onto NE Tolt Hill Road. Which lead to WA-203 N, straight into Carnation.

00:04:03, 00:04:02, 00:04:01...

As John entered Carnation the captain relayed some information: "John, the locals checked out the Issaquah coordinates. There was nothing, it was a decoy. The woman is in Carnation."

"10–4, almost there," John responded.

John turned onto Carnation Farm Road knowing the time was drawing near.

00:01:34, 00:01:33, 00:01:32...

Suddenly, the old Talbot barn came into sight, half a mile up on the left. John floored it as he approached the site and screeched to a halt just outside the barn, throwing up gravel and dirt in every direction. He glanced down at his wrist: *00:00:21, 00:00:20, 00:00:19...*

Ricky was out first, jumping down before the truck came to a stop. He rolled over, got up and ran towards the large doors leading inside the barn with John close on his heels. He crashed the door open and John flew past him into the open center on the structure. Just as his eyes could focus on the scene in front of him, he heard a loud gunshot. There is no mistaking the sound of a shotgun going off. The next sight that came to him was a lone woman, hanging from her shackled wrists, missing half her head.

John dropped to his knees with his head in his hands, knowing he was just seconds too late.

CHAPTER THREE

The feds showed up shortly after the shotgun shell hit the ground and they took control of the crime scene, which was fine with John and Ricky. They would go over the reports when they became available. As for now, John needed to get away from the site and attempt to erase the grisly image that was embedded in his mind. Photos would be taken, forensics would arrive and after all the evidence and data were collected, the body would be taken away for examination and identification.

On the ride back, not a word was uttered between the two men. They were both currently neck deep in grief and regret. Nothing hurts a cop more than failing to save a life that depended on them.

They returned to the station, and the captain met them as they walked in the door. "Heads up men, we did all that we could."

"With all due respect, sir, that's bullshit and you know it," John replied. "I'm going to the restaurant to get drunk. I'll be in tomorrow to go over the reports."

Captain Johnson patted John on the back and watched him walk out.

***

John downed his second whiskey as Red sat down next to him.

"Hey John, I heard what happened. You'll get him, you always do."

"Whatever happens now won't bring her back. She was an innocent woman, now gone forever, all because I failed."

"Yeah, you failed, but so did the feds, the captain and everyone else involved."

"Now I sit around and wait for that fucking nut to abduct someone else and go through the whole twisted process again. Why go through this charade? Why does he need to prove he's smarter than us, than me? I mean who the fuck cares?"

"You may find the answers when you find out who the killer is. It's definitely personal, John." Red said. "Do you have any idea who it could be? Someone you put away maybe?"

"I have no fucking idea, Red. None at all."

John ordered his third whiskey, ran his hand through his disheveled hair and leaned back on his barstool.

"That poor girl, she hung there for twenty-four hours knowing she was going to die, watching her life count down," John said. "Red, if you could know the exact time of your death beforehand, would you want to know?"

"Damn, that's a very complex question. I think the natural human reaction is yes, because we want to know everything, even if it's painful or difficult. That's why we gaze at accidents as we drive by; we can't look away. We have an instinct to uncover the unseen, to explore the unknown. However, I also think it would be wearisome living out the time we have left knowing when it was up, counting the days, the hours, the minutes..."

"Maybe, but it would also cause us to live the time we have left to the fullest. With limited time we would live without fear, and constantly exist in the moment."

"It's a complicated conception, my friend. I guess the effect would vary for everyone." He then patted John on the shoulder and went back to work as the rush of the late crowd began to arrive.

John's glance circled the restaurant, for the first time noticing that there were people around him. Sean lifted his beer in a salute from the other end of the bar. John gave a slight wave back and downed the rest of his whiskey.

Red drove John home, and as John got out he thanked his friend. He entered the house and was immediately welcomed at the door by Simba, wagging his tail and licking John's face as he settled down on one knee to pet and greet his companion. John thought it was moments like these that made owning a dog so enjoyable. No matter how terrible your day was, no matter how you may have fucked up, they always greeted you with the same love and excitement. That is what makes the vet bills, the accidents, the trips outside in the middle of the night, acceptable. That is the trade-off: unconditional loyalty and love.

John walked upstairs into Gianna's room. She was already asleep, so John sat down to watch her. As he gazed at her, she appeared to John as a young girl, donning her pajamas and a ponytail in her hair. A tear fell down his cheek as he noticed the innocence that his daughter still possessed. He dropped his head and brought his hands to his face. John cried for the woman who he failed to save that day. He cried for his daughter, gradually becoming a woman, and for the little girl he remembered. He cried for the pieces of his life he couldn't control, the evil overtaking the innocent, and the finality of death. He cried as time slowly, steadily, passed him by. In his mind, John pictured himself an old man with people who have gradually, but persistently, died around him, until one day he realizes everyone is gone. That is when you finally accept death without fear, because your life – or what mattered of it – had already been lived.

John opened his eyes and turned over as the bright, late morning sunshine invaded the dark sanctuary of his bedroom. He mumbled to himself and stumbled to the bathroom. He stood over the toilet and tried to hit the moving target in front of him. He had to shake off the residue of the previous evening's activities and make his way to the station. He showered, dressed, consumed two cups of black coffee and was on his way.

"Her name is Kerry Reid. They found her car abandoned, broken down on Beacon Ave near Jefferson Park," Captain Johnson said.

"Just like that, her car breaks down and she's gone forever," Ricky added.

"Was she married? Any children?" John asked.

"No, she was engaged. The feds talked to her fiancée this morning." The captain placed two files on the desk. "Here are your reports. I have to brief an officer in another case. Read up, ladies, and we'll regroup in a bit."

After a few minutes of scanning the report, John put the file down. "Anything here catch your eye?"

"Nope, nothing looks new. This guy is organized and efficient."

"He obviously puts his time in. He had to scout these sites beforehand. He knew they would be vacant and undisturbed for a couple of days."

"The property the barn is on was owned by the Talbots. The mortgage was foreclosed quite a while ago. The old man passed and the children weren't keeping up on the maintenance, or the bills. They all live out of state," Ricky said. "Everything this un-sub does is calculated."

"We have to dig into this file, figure out his methods, his profile, his next move before he does," John said.

"When I first hit the field in New York, a partner of mine had a saying: To stay ahead of a psychopath, you have to be willing to burrow into another man's soul. See what he sees. Feel what he feels. Think what he thinks."

"Your partner overlooked one small detail," John said.

"Yeah, what's that?"

"He assumed the man has a soul."

As the day grew long, John closed the file and leaned back in his chair ready to culminate the investigation for the evening. He started packing up his work as Ricky and Captain Johnson entered the office. Just as Ricky sat down his cell phone rang, followed by a couple of different tones.

"You answering that?" John asked.

"No, I let it go to voicemail."

"I respect the advancements in technology, but I've had my fill of all those beeps and tones constantly disturbing the peaceful quiet," John said.

"Technology is nothing to be afraid of. Welcome to 2018, gramps."

"The shiny new rookie even comes with a sense of humor. You learn that in the Big Apple, showboat?"

"Nope, I was born with it. You know what they say, 'if you can make a woman laugh, you will end up in bed with her,'" Ricky answered.

"Or, in your case, if you end up in bed with a woman, you will make her laugh."

The captain erupted in laughter and shortly after, both Ricky and John joined in. It was a much-needed release of tension for all three men.

That evening John took his family out to dinner. He needed to get his mind off the case and a quiet meal with his family was the perfect remedy. John smiled as the waitress took their orders. He looked around the table at his family and noticed how much his children had changed over the years. His son Ryann, now eleven, had started to become secretive and private. John knew puberty was just around the corner and communicating with both his children would become challenging.

"Ryann, when's your next baseball game?" he asked.

"Tomorrow night. Are you coming, Dad?"

"Of course I am."

"We're playing the first-place team, who's undefeated. They have Derek Fogarty pitching. He throws really hard. I'm not sure I can hit him."

John placed his glass of ice water down and looked at his children.

"I'm going to tell you both something, and I want you to listen up. There is nothing you cannot do if you possess the desire to achieve it. You will fail at times – we all fail at times in life – but what will make you a winner is getting back up and trying harder. Think about what you did wrong. Notice the little details that others may miss. Whether it be hitting a baseball, your schoolwork, or just being a better person. The effort you put forth is half the battle."

"But what if I can't hit him? What if it's too fast for me?"

"You will. Maybe not the first time, or even the second, but I promise you, keep trying and success will find you."

The food arrived just as John finished his fatherly pep talk and they all had an enjoyable dinner together.

John sat at his desk, reading a few emails when the captain's voice broke him out of his trance.

"John, come in here. He's at it again. Just got an email from him. The feed is loading now."

"Be right in," John said. As he walked into the captain's office, he noticed a strange look on his face. The captain looked like he had seen a ghost.

"John, hold on, don't look…"

John rushed around the desk to see what was on the screen. He froze in fear but couldn't pry his eyes from the horrid sight in front of him. In a clearing in a wooded area, with her head stuck in a guillotine, was his wife, Julie.

"*Noooo!*" he screamed.

"John, we'll get her out of there as soon as we get the hint. I will put every member on this team on it and call in the Marines if I have to—"

"Look!" John said and pointed to the bottom of the screen. *00:00:03, 00:00:02, 00:00:01...*

A split second before the blade fell and Julie's head was detached from her body, he saw his beautiful wife look up at the camera with tears running down her face. Her head rolled away, and blood spurted from her neck, soaking the ground below. John turned away and vomited.

He woke in a cold sweat and quickly turned to see Julie asleep beside him. He made his way to the bathroom and knelt in front of the toilet to finish the vomiting fit from his nightmare. He stood up and splashed cold water on his face and paused to look at his reflection. His eyes were bloodshot with an inflamed puffiness and dark circles around them. He dried off his face and went back to bed, hoping his dream would not return.

Red was stocking the bar, preparing for the lunchtime rush as Sean walked in and sat in his usual seat at the end of the bar.

"Hey, Red, how goes it?"

"Sean, aren't you working today?"

"I guess, but you can't drink all day if you don't start in the morning, my friend," He said with a laugh.

"I guess that means you want a drink. Brooklyn?"

"Well, if you are twisting my arm, what choice do I have?"

Red popped the cap off a fresh one and placed it in front of Sean.

"Hey Red, I've got a story for you."

"Okay, go ahead."

"My wife Debbie and I have a black Lab named Bailey. When we first got married, we lived in the city. I used to walk Bailey on the same route every day. I would stop off at four bars along the route. I called them the four corners. They would all let Bailey in with me and would give him a biscuit. I would get a beer at each one, so by the time the walk was over, I was feeling pretty well."

"Somehow, I find this story very believable up to this point," Red said.

"Oh, it is true, all of it. Anyway, one day I came down with the flu, so my wife took him on the usual route. When they approached each bar, Bailey pulled her right up to the door and wouldn't budge until he got his biscuit. When she got home she called me a useless drunk and told me I had lost dog-walking privileges. My dog, my best friend, told on me! You believe that shit?"

Red chuckled. "That's what you get for being a sneaky drunk."

Just as Sean was finishing his story, Matt walked in and sat next to him.

"Don't any of you slugs work?" Red asked.

"Work? I'm a teacher. Summers off. Plus, I went to Brown. Sean, did you know that?"

"I believe I heard you mention it once or twice."

"Oh, okay. I don't like to tell everyone that, so keep it between us, buddy."

"Buy me another beer and you got a deal, my scholarly friend."

"Red, I'll have a Brown University and another round for my friend here."

"A Brown University? Matt, I've been a bartender for close to twenty-five years and I've never heard of that."

"Seriously? It's one-part bourbon, one-part vermouth, and a couple dashes of orange bitters."

"Okay, I'll mix it up for you."

As Red served the next round, John walked in and sat at the other end of the bar.

"Hey, Red, am I interrupting?" John said as he glanced in the direction of Matt and Sean.

"Hell no, talking to those guys makes my brain cells commit suicide one at a time. How's the case going?"

"We're at a standstill until he reaches out to us again."

"Damn, that must be frustrating."

"He's a control freak who likes to play games and flaunt his self-proclaimed intelligence, especially towards me. If I can beat him at his own game, I may be able to knock him off balance and piss him off. Maybe then he stumbles and makes a mistake or two."

"How's Julie holding up?"

"She's onboard for now, but that can change quickly. Especially if she finds out I lied to her about my therapist's assessment."

"Never underestimate the power of estrogen, my friend. The female intuition has powers we can't begin to understand, especially if it is about something tied to their emotions. I guarantee she has a close eye on you."

"You're probably correct there, partner." John looked at the other end of the bar. Matt was ogling a young woman half his age as she walked by, headed to the ladies' room. Sean was lost in his beer. "How are things here?"

"Perfect, no issues at all."

"Glad to hear it. I really appreciate you covering for me, Red."

"I got your back, partner. Just find this a-hole."

The morning clouds dispersed and the warm, overcast day turned into a perfect evening for baseball. John sat between Julie and Gianna while holding Simba's leash as the malamute sprawled out on the cool grass under the bleachers. John watched Lucas Ferguson, the tall, twelve-year-old pitcher from the opposing team, warm up on the mound.

"John, he throws hard. I hope they can hit him," Julie said.

"Sure they can, if they go up to the plate with confidence," John replied. He noticed Ryann glance over at his family as he waited outside the dugout for the game to start.

Come on Ryann, you can do this, John thought as the umpire signaled it was time to play ball. Ryann struck out the first two times up and his team fell behind 2-0. After the second strikeout, John noticed his son glance at him on the way back to the dugout. John smiled and gave him a slight nod. He knew his son would understand the gesture as, *You got this.*

Heading into the final inning and still down two runs, Ryann was due up to bat third. Jimmy Collins walked and stole second as Gary Blake struck out. Ryann was up. The first pitch was a called strike, just over the outside corner at the knees. Julie grabbed John's hand and glanced at him with a concerned look in her eyes. The second pitch was in the dirt, and Jimmy advanced to third. The next pitch was right down the middle, and for the first time Ryann made contact against Lucas Ferguson. He fouled the ball over the opposing dugout down the first base line.

"That's it, Ryann! You can do it!" Julie yelled.

Ryann fouled off four more pitches and worked the count to 3-2. The next pitch was a hard fastball at the knees on the inside corner. Ryann finally got around on the ball and hit a line-drive down the line and over the third baseman's head. He rounded first and pulled into second as Jimmy trotted home. John felt an immense feeling of pride, and he pointed to his son standing on second base. The next batter struck out, ending the game, but, having overcome his doubts and fears, it was an experience Ryann would never forget.

A full day away from the case was just what John needed to recharge and refocus. He woke early, walked Simba, then showered and headed to the station. While pulling in, he noticed the absence of the captain's car. He then entered the station, noticing the deafening silence. John headed to the dispatch office. As he entered he waved at Rosalie, the part-time dispatcher who had started working at the station over fifteen years ago.

"John!" she said as she hung up the phone. "So nice to see you. How have you been? How's Julie? The children? I bet they're big.

What are they now, ten and twelve? I heard you were back to work on the new case. Any progress? Damn shame about that woman. Want some coffee? I just brewed a new pot."

"Hi, Rosalie, which question would you like me to answer first?" John said with a polite smile on his lips.

"Aw, I'm sorry. Sometimes I get carried away when I get excited. It's so nice to see you again. Plus, I'm not used to people listening to me; my husband, my children, the 9-1-1 callers..."

"A wise man once told me, 'If you want to be heard more, speak less,'" John said.

"Really? I'll have to try that... tomorrow," she said with a wink.

"Well, to answer your questions, everything is fine, thank you. How are Jason and the kids?"

"I can't complain, although I still may."

"Has the captain or Ricky Barnes been in?"

"Both are due in shortly," she replied.

"Okay, great. I'll go over the case files while I wait for them."

"If you need anything, don't be shy. There's fresh coffee and I stocked the kitchen fridge with some goodies."

"Thank you, I'm good for now. I'll be at my desk solving the world's problems."

"I noticed you even got your old desk back, good for you."

"Temporarily," John replied.

"Hey, you never know. It may be permanent."

John smiled and walked out of the control room, placed his briefcase on his desk and sat down. A few minutes later Ricky Barnes walked in and sat down across from him. "Hey, John. Good morning."

"Hey, long night?"

"Not really, although I did have a date."

"Yeah? How did it go?" John asked.

"I think it is safe to say it wasn't a love connection."

"That's too bad. How long have you been on the prowl?"

"Hmmm, about six months. I had a steady thing with Kim, but we decided to split."

"Why?"

"She wanted to get married, have children, get a house, the whole nine yards. I wasn't ready."

"Has she moved on?"

"Yup, she's dating a dude named Larry."

"Larry? Seriously?" John asked.

"As serious as a broken condom."

"People actually name their children Larry?"

"Well, I assume Lawrence, but it always becomes Larry. I thought it was just a name Hollywood used in movies when all the other names were used up. You see them in the credits after the film is over. Larry, fifth stranger on the street. Gertrude, the third waitress in the cafe. Elmer, the gas station attendant. Bertha, the woman on the park bench. You get the idea. Well, come to find out these are actually real names, and Larry is at the top of the list."

"Wow, who knew?" John said. "What's the dude like? Have you met him?"

"Nope, but I assume he's what you would think a Larry would be; the uncle who wears the Hawaiian shirt and insists on working the grill at family cookouts. He's the dude who tries to win the family volleyball game by spiking the ball at his ten-year-old niece, then makes his brother's pretty wife a drink with an extra shot of alcohol, hoping she gets tipsy and flashes a breast at some point. That's Larry. A great guy... not creepy at all."

The captain walked into the hysterical laughter of Ricky and John.

"Glad to see you two getting along so well. Team chemistry is very important. Now, what's so funny?"

When John was able to catch his breath he said, "Some dude named Larry is banging Ricky's ex-girlfriend."

"Larry? I thought that was a fake name?" the captain said as he glanced toward Ricky as the two detectives continued their howling.

Ricky said, "This nut-job is an enigma. He or she has no discernable style, victim preference, or pattern. Maybe that's the point. Maybe he understands data can be uncovered through patterns or styles, Data that can help us uncover his or her secrets."

"It's he, Ricky. I'm certain," John said with confidence.

"Well until you have proof of gender, I'll accept both as possibilities, old wise one."

"You do realize to be old and wise, someone had to start out young and stupid. That is the level you currently reside at," John replied.

"Okay ladies, ease up a bit. Going at each other's throats isn't going to help us solve this case. The feds are just as much in the dark as we are. You pair are the best detectives I have ever worked with, so let's combine our talents and individual strengths and solve this thing before the feds do."

Ricky looked up at Captain Johnson. "Is that what is most important to you, beating the feds to the punch?"

"Of course not. I want to keep my citizens safe at any cost. That is my first priority. However, solving it before the feds would be a nice bonus."

"The problem is, all we can do is sit here and wait for him to make the next move," Ricky said.

"Him? You're learning rookie," John said.

The dark figure watched over the Corbin residence as Julie Corbin pulled into the driveway with her two children in tow. As she exited the vehicle, he watched as a warm breeze caused wisps of her ash brown hair to flutter.

John, what a beautiful wife you have, he thought. His eager gaze followed the trio as they entered the house.

December 22, 1999
John Corbin rushed into Harbor View Medical Hospital, approached the front desk and asked where Tabatha Jones was.

"Tabatha Jones? The gunshot wound? Officer...?"

"Corbin, John Corbin. I was first on the scene."

The nurse looked up and their eyes met for the first time.

"I understand, Mr. Corbin. Ms. Jones is in surgery, she has lost quite a bit of blood."

"Will she live?"

"I'm sorry Mr. Corbin—"

"Please call me John."

"Okay, John. We still don't know yet."

"She has to. I promised her. She's only ten."

"How do you know that?"

"I asked her age while I held her wound together waiting for the ambulance. She has a younger brother who looks up to her. She was afraid to leave him."

The nurse held John's gaze for a few seconds, digesting John's statement. "My name is Julie, John. Let me see if there's any information I can find out for you."

John smiled. "Thank you, Julie."

He watched the nurse walk down the hall and through the double doors that lead to the operating room. A few minutes later, she appeared and approached him.

"I'm sorry, it's shaky. I want to be honest with you, we're not certain she's going to pull through.

John lowered his head and brought a hand to his face, attempting to hold back tears. Julie kept her eyes on him as a lone teardrop fell down his cheek.

"John, did you know her, I mean before tonight?"

"No."

"It's touching that you care so much. It's something I don't see here often, officers so emotional."

"I promised her. She's just an innocent little girl who was in the wrong place at the wrong time. Fucking drug dealers."

Julie walked around the counter and hugged him. "This is for letting me know that men like you still exist."

As John hugged her back, her soft touch and sweet vanilla scent invaded his senses. He released her and stepped back. "I know you're busy. I'm going to sit and wait, but please let me know of any updates. I'm not leaving until she pulls through."

"Of course. I'll inform you as soon as I hear anything."

"Thank you," John said as he retreated to the waiting room and collapsed on an oversized chair. He knew he had a long interlude ahead of him, and as he replayed the night's tragic events in his mind, his eyes grew heavy and he drifted off.

"John, wake up."

He opened his eyes and stared into the biggest, deepest brown eyes he had ever seen. "Julie? How... what?" He jumped up and looked at the clock.

"It's okay, relax. You slept for a few hours."

"Tabatha, how is she?"

Julie smiled. "She made it, she's going to be fine."

Julie wrapped her arms around John and he felt her heartbeat against his chest. Her soft hair tickled his neck and he felt an intense jolt of passion flow through his body.

"Thank you, can I see her?"

"Not now, possibly tomorrow. She needs rest tonight. I, however, would like to treat you to some food."

"Aren't you still working?"

"No, my shift ended twenty minutes ago. I stayed to give you the good news."

"Thank you, I guess the least I can do is buy you dinner then," John said.

"Nope, my treat. After witnessing the brutality people hand down on each other, you have singlehandedly rekindled my faith in the human race."

Julie took John by the hand and led him out of the hospital.

***

Julie set the table and called the children for dinner. Ryann hurried in and sat in his usual chair as Julie placed the roast in the center of the table, flanked by baked potatoes and butternut squash.

"I'm starving!" Ryann said as he grabbed a potato and a scoop of squash.

"Of course you are, but let's wait for Gianna to join us before we start."

"Is dad eating with us?"

"No, he's at the station. He'll be home in a bit but he told us not to wait."

Gianna walked in and sat down at the table.

"How would you two like to walk Simba after we eat? He'd love to get out in this nice weather."

"Okay, can I play video games online after?" Ryann asked.

"For an hour, then do something constructive."

"Mom, saving the earth from the evil alien race *is* constructive."

"Sure it is, Ryann. How would you like to play a board game later? Maybe Daddy will be home in time to join us."

"Monopoly!" Ryann said.

"Clue!" Gianna countered.

"After you clean your rooms, maybe we will have time to play both games."

After dinner, Gianna secured Simba's harness and led him out into the front yard with Ryann by her side.

"Don't go far, just around the block," Julie called after them.

"Okay, Mom," Gianna replied.

Simba's tongue hung out as he became joyful and animated, anticipating his walk. The children happily lead their large pet down the front walk and turned left, heading south.

The dark figure watched as the two Corbin children burst through the front door and down the walk with their dog. He waited until they had progressed down the street before exiting the vehicle. He tracked them from the opposite side until they reached the end and turned left around a wooded bend. He turned around and retreated in the opposite direction. He paused when he reached his black SUV and waited with his eyes riveted on the far corner. A crisp breeze gave the budding night an electric feel. He glanced up as the last bit of sun fell behind the trees on the horizon, turning the rising moon red.

"Can I hold his leash?" Ryann asked his older sister as they continued down Pine Ridge Street.

"Okay, but just for a bit. He's very strong."

"I'm stronger than you, Gianna. I can handle him."

Gianna handed Ryann the leash as they approached the corner of their street. The sun had departed from the horizon and the moon was now dominant in the Seattle night sky.

"If he stops, let him find his spot."

"His spot for what?"

"What do you think, genius?" Gianna said.

"Oh, that. Yuk."

"Hey, you wanted to hold him. I should make you scoop it into the bag too."

"No way, I'm not old enough for that. You do it."

They turned left around the corner and past a wooded lot as headlights appeared behind them. The vehicle pulled to a stop as the children turned to see who it was. The headlights blinded them as the driver got out and walked toward them.

"Dad!" Ryann yelled as he dropped the leash and ran to his father.

"Hey buddy, hi sweetheart," John said as he hugged his son. Gianna picked up the leash and held Simba who was pulling her toward her father.

"Hi dad," she said.

"Mom said we can play games tonight."

"Okay then, that's what we'll do. I'll follow you guys home. Did you eat dinner?"

"Yes! Roast, potatoes, and squash."

"Sounds yummy. Go on, I'll be right behind you."

The dark figure watched John Corbin escort his children home, park his truck in the driveway, and happily enter his house, fulfilled and content. *Something has to be done about that,* he thought as he climbed into his SUV. He paused long enough to glance at the house one last time. He saw through the window John hug and kiss his wife as she handed him a plate of hot food.

"Until we meet again Mr. Corbin," he said to himself as he drove away.

Red stood behind the bar as he looked over the restaurant. The dinner crowd had come and gone, and the evening settled into a slow but steady stream of late eaters and drunks.

"Damn, someone needs a ride," Sean said as he glanced at his phone. "Oh well, someone else can get them." He chuckled and hit the screen off mode on his phone.

"How do you make money if you always refuse to give people rides?" Red asked.

"I don't always refuse, only when I'm busy drinking."

"Like I said, how do you make money if you always refuse to give people rides?"

Artie walked in and sat down next to Sean. "Hey, guys."

"What's up, Artie?" Sean asked.

"Well, I wrote my lovely wife Gina a poem."

"Seriously? Do you sport a vagina?"

Artie smirked. "What? No, I just like to show her my inner feelings sometimes."

"Okay, let's see it."

Artie reluctantly pulled out a piece of paper and handed it to Sean.

"Can I get you a drink?" Red asked.

"Sure, I'm going to hit it hard tonight, the wife is out. I'll have a Malibu cocktail."

After the thirty seconds it took Red to figure out it wasn't a joke, he walked away to prepare the drink.

"Did you just order a Malibu? What the fucks wrong with you, dude?" Sean said. He shook his head and looked down to read the poem:

Like an angel sent from above, you fit me like a glove.

Will you really be my last love?

I was blindsided, you repaired my wounded heart with a tender patch.

The day we met was game, set, and match.

When I breathe you in, you fill me with glee.

I will always love you, G.

Sean's face turned green as he dropped the paper. "I think I'm going to be sick," he said as he ran to the bathroom.

"Fuck's up with him?" Red asked.

"Maybe he drank too much," Artie said as he quickly scooped up the paper and slipped it in his pocket. "Poor guy isn't man enough to hold his liquor."

"I would never have guessed that. Here's your Malibu."

"Thanks, how's business?"

"It's been steady since we opened. We really pick up in the summer," Red replied.

"Hey, isn't your partner John a cop? Isn't he handling the Seattle Slayer case?"

"Pardon? Seattle Slayer?"

"That's what the press is calling him. How is the investigation going?"

"Ah, well... not too well as far as I know. John hasn't discussed it with me. But he's still out there, so watch your back."

"I told my wife Gina to be aware of everything around her. She's the love of my life and if anything happened to her I'd be crushed."

"Yeah, I think we all get that," Red said as Sean returned to his seat looking refreshed.

"What the heck happened to you? Too many drinks?" Red asked.

"Huh? No way. Read this dude's poem and you'll understand."

"I'll pass, thank you."

"What? Is it that bad? It rhymes," Artie said.

"Bad? Dude, let's just say if you dropped your drawers right now to reveal a pink clitoris I wouldn't be shocked, or even surprised for that matter."

"You don't appreciate art," Artie said.

"You wouldn't know art if smacked you in your G-spot, my friend. On that note, grab me another beer, Red. I'm going to drink that poem out of my head."

"Coming right up," Red said as Artie shook his head and took a sip of his Malibu.

Early the next morning, John arrived at the station. As he sat back in his chair with his favorite book opened, he took a quick glance out the window and noticed Ricky approaching. He entered the station and sat down across from John, greeting him with a nod.

"What are you reading?" Ricky asked.

"The Fountainhead."

"Do people still read physical books? You've never heard of an e-book, grandpa?"

"I have, but I like the real thing. There is something to be said for the feel of the soft page in my hand, the earthy scent, and the ability to add it to a collection in my bookcase when finished. Not to mention I prefer not to stare at another electronic screen for hours on end. Physical pages are easier on the eyes."

"There're many benefits to reading e-books; it's cheaper, it's instantly obtainable, and it's green. Don't you care about the environment, old man?"

"We can plant more trees. Does everything we own today have to come with beeps, lights, and tones?"

"So, what's it about?" Ricky asked, changing the subject.

"You've never read it?"

"I only read non-fiction."

"Well, I've read this book five times," John replied.

"Why, does the content change each time you read it?"

"I don't read it hoping for something different. I read it to be in that universe again, to experience the characters and the story again. As a matter of fact, each time I read it I feel the sadness of knowing it is coming to an end as I approach the final scenes."

"So, what's so great about that particular book?"

"It makes me feel good to be alive. It resurrects my faith in humanity and what we can achieve. It cleanses and purifies my soul."

"You get all that from a fictional story?" Ricky asked.

"I do. You should borrow it and give it a try."

John noticed Ricky glance down at the cover, the naked man holding what looked to be the sun in his bare hand. For a moment, John thought Ricky contemplated picking it up and taking his recommendation. But the thought was gone as quickly as it came as Ricky smirked and looked up at John.

"I'll pass for now, but maybe sometime in the future."

"Sure, I'll leave it here. Just take it whenever you'd like to read it. Remember, in youth we learn, with age we understand."

"What do you mean by that?"

"When we're young, our brains understand black and white, statistics and definite, rational certainties we learn from life. As we age, we understand the grey areas, the emotions and the abstract details that also come from life. The wise combine both to have a better understanding of our world. Sometimes reading good fiction helps uncover and fill in those cracks."

"Speaking of abstract details, anything new on the Seattle Slayer?" Ricky asked.

John looked up at Ricky and flinched. "So, you've heard that horrible nickname as well? Comparing this lunatic to that amazing horse is a travesty."

"Well, I think it's more a play on words than any type of comparison."

"Maybe, but it's still wrong. We have nothing new. Where, when or how he strikes again is anyone's guess."

"I'll be heading out for a bit. I have to grab a report at the morgue but I'll be back this afternoon. Call me if anything comes up."

"Will do. I'm grabbing a coffee," John said as he got up and headed for the cafeteria. When he returned with a cup of joe, Ricky was gone, along with the book.

The dark figure sipped his gin and tonic as he noticed a man at the end of the bar drinking alone. He had grey hair with a matching beard, maybe 5'8", 150 pounds. *Loner, mid-sixties,* he thought. The man looked desolate and depressed, as if he were attempting to drink his loneliness away. He continued to watch the man down three scotches in rapid succession and stumble to the bathroom. The dark figure glanced around the bar, noticing the vacancy, then noticed the bartender who was having a conversation with his cell phone. *Not a man who remembers details,* he thought as the inebriated man returned, dropped a twenty on the bar, and headed out the door. The dark figure took one last sip of his drink, placed the empty glass down on the bar, and followed him.

CHAPTER FOUR

The last coherent memory Brian Simmons had was finishing his last scotch, leaving the bar, and heading through the back alley toward his apartment on 13th Avenue behind the University. Then he woke up here, standing in a large glass tank that came up to his shoulders, with his arms chained and secured above his head with the aftereffects of his binge from the night before pounding in his head. *Where the fuck am I?* he thought as he glanced at his surroundings. He was in a small wooden room brightened by a single lightbulb hanging directly above his head.

"Help!" he yelled, noticing the lone door leading into the six-by-eight-foot room. He looked up at the ceiling where his wrists were secured to hooks and anchored into wooden beams that ran horizontally across the structure. He noticed something that sent a chill up his spine, and terror through his heart. Below his feet, under the glass floor of the tank, was a small flame attached to a hose leading to a propane tank in the corner. He then noticed a spigot hanging over the far wall of the tank with a garden hose attached, leading through a hole in the wall. Suddenly, the spigot came to life and a rush of water flowed into the tank. As the water crept up his body, the reality of what was about to happen sent him into a panic.

"No, Christ no!" he screeched as the water reached his knees. "Somebody fucking help me!" The cold water continued to inch its way up his body.

The dark figure watched his new quarry panic as the water crept up his legs, then his waist, then his chest. Satisfied, he then turned the water pressure off from his control room. The man stood there with his arms secured above his head anxiously looking around, the water level settling just under his shoulders. *Just like a rodent caught in a trap,* the dark figure thought as he studied his prey's actions. Finally, the man's cold grey eyes noticed the camera and the dark figure stared directly at his captive through the computer screen.

"Just sit back and relax, old man. We all meet our maker at some point. Be happy I've given you this privilege before your time," he said to himself. "Now, I will leave you alone for a bit. I have work to get to. Rest up, for the show is about to start and you are the main attraction, the star of the production."

He flipped off the camera and opened his secure email account, entering the name Captain Michael Johnson. Before he started typing, he sat back and gazed at the screen as an evil smirk played on his lips.

The late afternoon sun was starting its descent across the Seattle horizon as John glanced out the window of the station.

"Looks like it's going to be another beautiful evening," he said to Ricky. "Any plans?"

"No, I had a date last night, so I'm just going to hang in and watch the game."

The captain walked up to John's desk, catching the last of this conversation. "Another date? How did this one go?" he asked.

"Ugh."

"Ugh? Care to elaborate?"

Ricky looked from the captain to John then back to the captain again.

"Sure. It was my third date with Gabrielle. Spent a hundred on dinner and spent another fifty on drinks and dancing after."

"Gabrielle? Cool name," John said.

"Yeah well, I've started calling her Gabby cause the broad doesn't shut up. Anyway, on the way home, she leans over, undoes my pants and gives me head as I'm driving."

"No shit. Did you pull over?" Captain Johnson asked.

"I had to. I pulled over on a side street and she finished."

"Well, at least you got a blowjob out of it."

"Fuck the blowjob. The best part was the fifteen minutes of silence," Ricky said which brought plenty of laughter from his two colleagues.

"I'm glad you two are enjoying yourselves. Needless to say, there won't be a fourth date. How did you guys do it? How did you find a wife that was right for you? It seems an impossible task."

"At some point, it'll just happen. You won't have to second guess yourself, you'll just know instinctually," John said. "My advice is not to search for her. She'll come at a time when you least expect it."

"Yeah, well someday I guess," Ricky said.

"Listen to this man, Ricky. I remember when he was in the same situation you're in now and look how he turned out. Husband of the year material," Captain Johnson said as he walked away and headed to his office.

John looked at Ricky. "Well, I wouldn't go that far, but Julie and I do okay."

"Meanwhile, there are worse things in life than sleeping with a different woman every month," Ricky said. "I'm going to pack it in and call it a day. The Mariners, Chinese takeout, and a few beers await me."

As soon as Ricky made his first step towards the door, Captain Johnson burst out of his office. "Come in here you two! It's on. I have a new email."

***

The three cohorts gathered around the computer as the captain opened his email. John noticed a quick glance from the captain as he clicked on the message. All that it contained was a hyperlink for a video feed. The captain pasted the link into his browser, sat back and waited for the fateful scene to come to life. The video feed opened and instantly they were viewing an older man, maybe in his sixties, standing in a glass tank of water. His arms were secured to the ceiling. The water line was just under his shoulders.

"Shit, is he going to drown him? Dunk his head under?" Ricky asked.

"No, look underneath," the captain said as he brought the cursor over the spot and magnified it. "There's a small flame under the vat that connects to a propane tank in the corner. He's going to boil him alive like a fucking lobster."

They all took a moment to regain their composure as the reality of the situation sank in; if they couldn't save him, this man was going to die a horrific death.

"Okay, let's start from the beginning. What kind of room or structure is he in?" John said.

"It's all wooden. Looks like maybe a room in a cabin or even a shed," Ricky said.

"My guess is a shed. It's very compact, maybe six by eight. What rooms are that small, even in a cabin? Also, the rafters are untreated two-inch by six-inch planks, it looks like. Most cabins use treated logs cut down to fit the size of the cabin. I bet my pecker this is a shed."

"Okay, so we have a six by eight-foot shed. Gee, that really narrows it down to any butt-fuck town, U.S.A," Ricky said.

"I'm going to send the link to the feds... have them run a search on this guy's face. If we can figure out who he is, it will give us an idea where he was abducted," the captain said.

The captain left John and Ricky and headed to the office next door to speak with the feds.

The pair continued to survey the scene, looking for anything that may give them a clue as to who the man is or where he was being held.

"John, you have no idea who this maniac could be? I mean, he asked for you personally. There has to be some connection."

"I have no idea. Someone I put away at some point, or maybe a family member of someone I put away? That's always possible."

"That may be the missing link to solving this whole thing and finding this lunatic."

"I know. Believe me, I've thought about it many times but I have no idea."

"Look at that poor guy. I can't imagine hanging there for twenty-four hours to be boiled to death. He may be insane long before then," Ricky remarked sadly.

"Have the nightmares started yet? Do you see faces that you're unable to save?"

Ricky glanced quickly at John then back to the computer screen.

"Yes. Does it get worse?"

"I'm not going to lie, each case you fail to solve, each person you fail to save, will haunt you forever. It doesn't get easier, but over time you'll learn how to deal with it. You'll learn how to flip that switch off. Sure, those thoughts and images will invade your dreams, but you'll learn how to put it all aside and function during the days just as I have."

Ricky and John turned their attention back to the scene. The man looked at the camera with a defeated, morbid look on his face.

John glanced at Ricky, who seemed transfixed on the man standing in the tank. "Do you think he's more consumed with dying, or the pain he will feel before?" Ricky asked.

John inhaled deeply as he worried about the changes he started to see in his young partner. "I'm sure both equally," John answered.

Let those thoughts go, he pleaded in his own head. *Stay clear of that path, for once you go down it, you will never be the same.*

***

22:51:03, 22:51:02, 22:51:01...

"The feds have a good shot of the victim's face. They're going to run it through their database using their NGI software," Captain Johnson said as he walked back into the office. "They'll then review the candidate's photos and perform a further investigation to determine if any of the candidate's photos match. Let's hope the vic has a record."

"Now what do we do other than sitting here, watching this poor bastard?" Ricky asked.

"Pray, I guess," the captain answered.

"What if I don't believe in prayer?" John asked. "I was never one for church. I'd rather be in the mountains thinking about God than be in church thinking about the mountains."

"Good point. Sarah wouldn't hear of me not joining her, but I'm not sure I get any comfort from it anymore. I've seen too much evil in my life," the captain said.

"That makes two of us," John said.

John glanced at Ricky and noticed he was still studying the video feed. John couldn't tell if he was searching for clues or if he was still digesting the morbid actuality of the situation. He looked at the captain and motioned for him to meet him in the kitchen.

John walked out of the office, through the station, and entered the kitchen. He poured himself a cup of coffee and Captain Johnson soon appeared.

"What is it, John?"

"We need to watch him," John said as he motioned towards the office. "This all may be getting to him. He's acting a bit off, saying strange things. He's very green and we don't want to burn him out. Think about giving him a week after this one; he'll need a break."

The Captain frowned. "I've noticed it as well. I was going to mention it to you and get your opinion. At least now I know it wasn't my imagination. After we save this guy, *if* we save this guy, I'll tell him to take a week. Thanks, John."

20:25:03, 20:25:02, 20:25:01...

John was alone in the breakroom working on his second piece of pepperoni pizza when Captain Johnson rushed into the room.

"We have a name. Brian Simmons from Capitol Hill. He was picked up for public intoxication and urination in last year. He lives on 13th Avenue in an apartment complex between Seattle Central College and Squire Park."

"I know the neighborhood. I'll take Ricky and comb the area for info."

"Okay, I'll call the owner and have him meet you there with the key. Contact me with any and all info you collect."

"Will do," John said as he grabbed Ricky and headed out the door.

19:33:03, 19:33:02, 19:33:01...

John pulled up to the complex on 13th Avenue where Brian Simmons lived. He glanced at Ricky. "Ready, partner?"

"Let's go," Ricky replied.

"He lives on the second floor, apartment 2C."

John led Ricky to the front door where an old man waited. John noticed the man's short, squat physique, his white hair and pale blue eyes. A friendly smile appeared as the man stepped forward with his right hand held out in an offer to shake.

"John Corbin? My name is Tom Ford. Captain Johnson called and informed me of Mr. Simmons abduction. I'll help in any way I can, just tell me what you need."

John shook his hand. "Thank you, Mr. Ford. This is my partner, detective Ricky Burton."

John waited as the two men shook hands and exchanged pleasantries.

"We'll need to get into Mr. Simmons apartment, and will need to ask you a few questions about him."

"Absolutely, follow me."

The building was an old three-story complex in need of maintenance. There was one bathroom on each floor shared by the occupants of four one-room apartments. John made a mental note not to touch anything for fear of picking up unwanted bacteria.

"He lived in 2C, second floor," Mr. Ford said.

They followed him up a narrow, dingy spiraling staircase to the second landing.

"Here we are, his room is down the hall to the left, right after the bathroom."

When they reached the door, Tom inserted his key and opened it. The pungent odor of sweat, mold, and alcohol hit John immediately. Tom stepped aside, and John led the way into the room. To his left was an old black leather couch riddled with tears and worn spots. There were a pillow and blanket which obviously completed Mr. Simmons sleeping arrangement. Straight ahead against the far wall was a sink with a modest table in front of it. To the right were a leather chair, a small television on a stand, and a framed picture on the wall. John walked over to inspect the image. It contained a photo of a younger Brian Simmons standing beside a beautiful young woman.

"Who is this standing next to Mr. Simmons?" John asked.

"I believe that is his daughter, Alexis."

"Daughter? Do you have any info on her, address or phone number?"

"I may. Let me check my office," Tom answered as he turned and left the room.

"I wonder why we had no record of a daughter," John said to Ricky.

"That's strange. Our boy is a drinker. Three empty bottles in the sink. Hey, check this out."

John walked over and glanced at something hanging on the wall by the sink.

"That's a Medal of Honor. He's a war hero."

"Nam?"

"Had to be."

Tom returned with a piece of paper he handed to John.

Alexis Carson, 500 Elliot Ave West, unit 410

"Thank you. Did you know Mr. Simmons served?" John asked.

"I saw the medal but never discussed it with him. He's a loner, doesn't talk much and when he does, it's never about himself."

"Okay, any of the neighbors available?"

"You can try the doors but they're probably drunk, high, or both. Even if they aren't, they wouldn't be much help to you. They keep to themselves and don't pay attention to each other."

"Okay, we're all set here. Thank you, Tom. You've been a great help."

John glanced at the door across the hall labeled 2D, walked over and knocked. No answer. He continued down the hall to 2B and repeated the process. John heard someone move on the inside, so he knocked again, harder this time.

"Go the fuck away!" someone yelled.

John glanced at 2A, shook his head and walked out.

19:01:03, 19:01:02, 19:01:01...

"Ricky, I called into the station to check on the Mr. Simmons' military service. Brian Simmons won the Medal of Honor in the Vietnam War. He's a hero."

"Now he's forgotten by the world and the country he served. Just doesn't seem right. So where does his daughter live?" Ricky asked as they got into John's truck.

"Elliot Ave West, Lower Queen Anne, just west of the needle."

"Right off the bay?"

"The same. you're learning, rookie."

A few minutes later John pulled up in front of unit 410. "Let's go."

"John, maybe you should take this one solo. Having two detectives grilling her for info may intimidate her. We need her as relaxed as possible. Use that old-fashioned charm," Ricky said.

John sat in the driver's seat and glanced at the front door. "You may be right. You go alone. I think some contemporary youthful charm may work better. I'll call the captain and brief him."

Ricky glanced at John. "Okay, I'll go."

Moments later, Ricky knocked on the front door and waited. The door opened slowly and only as far as the chain lock would allow. Ricky gazed into the most beautiful set of sea green eyes he had ever seen.

"May I help you?" the owner of the eyes asked.

"Alexis Carson?"

"Yes."

Ricky held up his badge. "I'm Detective Barnes. May I come in and ask you a few questions about your father?"

Alexis looked at Ricky a second too long before dropping her eyes to the ground.

"What's this about?" she asked.

"Ma'am, your father's been abducted."

Alexis glanced back up at Ricky, shut the door, undid the chain and let him in.

He followed her to a couch just off the front foyer.

"Have a seat. Drink?"

"Water is fine, thank you."

As she left the room, Ricky glanced at her laptop still open in front of the couch on the coffee table. He had obviously interrupted her.

She returned with two bottles of water. After she handed one to Ricky she asked, "Now, what has the useless drunk gotten himself into this time?"

"Thank you. Have I interrupted you?" Ricky asked as he took the bottle of water and pointed towards the computer.

"No. Well, yes, but that's okay. You obviously have something serious to discuss."

He let out a sigh, took a sip of water and said, "Your father has been abducted and is being held hostage."

"By who? Where?"

"We don't know either of those answers yet. We've received a video feed of him in restraints. We're working on uncovering who, where, and why." Ricky looked Alexis in the eyes with a sincere look on his face. "Anything you can tell me about him will help us figure it out."

"I don't talk to him. He left my mother and me when I was four. I hardly remember him. He left us for the bottle. I'm sorry detective Burton..."

"Call me Ricky."

"I'm sorry, Ricky, but I'm not sure I can help you."

"Is there anything you remember, anything your mother may have said?"

"Well, I remember one thing. It was the reason he left us, a bar he used to hang out at called The Ba Bar."

Ricky clicked his pen opened his notebook. "I'm sorry, I just transferred here from New York, the Bar Bar? B-A-R?"

Alexis smiled, presenting a beautiful set of straight, white teeth. Ricky noticed how captivating but innocent her smile was, and he returned the grin.

"B-A, Ba Bar, on 12th Avenue. It's attached to a Vietnamese Restaurant."

Ricky froze and looked up, "Vietnamese? That's strange. Maybe it's a way for him to face and overcome his demons."

"Demons, what do you mean?" Alexis asked.

Ricky looked up and studied Alexis' green eyes and suddenly knew. "Alexis, did you know your father served in Nam and won the Medal of Honor?"

"What? But how? My mother never told me that."

"There may be some things you and your mom need to discuss. It seems she might not have been totally honest with you. I'm sorry."

Alexis put her hand over her mouth and Ricky could see the confusion and hurt in her eyes.

"Listen, maybe you should come down to the station. We can help you uncover your father's real story."

"You're willing to do that for me?"

Ricky smiled. "Sure." He reached into his pocket and took a card from his wallet. He then wrote his personal cell number on the back. "Here, call me anytime. Now, I need to look into this bar and see if I can uncover any info on your dad."

Alexis walked Ricky to the door and as he stepped through the threshold. Alexis said, "Detective Burton..."

Ricky turned, and Alexis placed her arms around him. "Thank you, Ricky."

Ricky gently hugged her back and walked to John's truck.

18:34:03, 18:34:02, 18:34:01...

"What was that?" John said with a smirk.

"What was what?"

"The hug?"

"Oh, she was just thanking me."

"Thanking you for what?"

"It's a long story. The good news is I know where her father hangs out."

"Great... shoot."

"The Ba Bar."

"You're kidding."

"Nope, you know it?"

"Yes, it's attached to a Vietnamese restaurant," John said as he pulled out and headed for the bar.

"That's the one."

"That's really strange, why the hell would he drink there?"

"My guess is it helps him overcome his demons. Maybe he feels bad for what he had to do in the war."

"While you were in there flirting, I did some research. He entered the war in 1970 at the age of eighteen, a few years before Nixon pulled us out in '73. He's sixty-five today, so he must have been forty or so when he had Alexis."

"So, he serves for three years, becomes a war hero, comes home and functions well enough for twenty years to meet a woman and have a child, then just falls apart?"

"Ricky, we can't begin to understand how the trauma and stress of war affects veterans. For some it may be immediate, while others it may take years, gradually building up inside until living with reality becomes unfathomable."

"What are you, an expert on PTSD?" Ricky asked.

John looked ahead at the road for a moment in silence then replied, "Let's just say I have a bit of history with it. It comes with the job."

John pulled into the parking lot of their destination. The pair walked into the lounge and sat at the bar, which was empty except for a pair of working men in painter's clothes seated at the other end.

"May I help you, gentlemen?"

"What's your name?" John asked.

"Doug Stevens."

John looked at the bartender, gave him a friendly smile, and placed a picture on the bar top. "Hi Doug, do you know this man?"

He picked it up and quickly glanced at it. John saw the immediate recognition in his eyes.

"Sure, that's Brian. Not sure of his last name. He's been coming here, drinking his sorrows away for years. He was in here last night, actually."

John glanced at Ricky, looked back at the bartender and asked, "Was he with anyone?"

"No, he's always alone. Sometimes he'll talk a bit to me or other patrons, but he's always alone. Is everything okay?"

"At this time, yes. Did you see anyone talk to him last night?"

"No, it was pretty empty when he was here, although there was one other dude. He left immediately after Brian did."

"Did he look suspicious, like he was interested in Brian?" John asked.

"I really didn't notice. He abruptly downed a gin and tonic and was gone. Left a great tip, though."

"What did this man look like?" Ricky asked.

"You know, it's hard to remember. He was the type that sort of just blends in. Short, dark hair, square jaw, kinda handsome."

Ricky flipped open his notebook. "Height, weight?"

"5'10", 180 pounds maybe. That's just a guess."

"Clothes?"

"Pretty nondescript. Old jeans, black boots, flannel shirt. That's all I can remember."

John nodded and closed his small notebook. "Okay, here's my card. If you think of anything else or see this man in here again, please give me a call."

"You got it."

John and Ricky stood up and headed to the door. After a few steps, Doug called out to them. "I do remember one other feature."

John turned and looked at Doug. "What is it?"

"His eyes were dark and cold, without feeling."

Ricky glanced at John and the partners walked out.

17:22:03, 17:22:02, 17:22:01...

John and Ricky were back at the station, waiting to debrief Captain Johnson on the info they uncovered. The press had gotten wind of another victim and came to the station to press for information and answers.

"He's going to be one grumpy captain when he gets in here, mark my word. He hates answering to the press," John said.

"I don't blame him, fucking parasites. How did they find out?"

"Who the heck knows. The feds aren't as buttoned up as you would think. People talk."

"Well, it's a good thing he's a grounded, secure, professional man. Any less and they may get to him."

"Years of experience and success has eliminated any self-doubt he may have had, trust me."

"Is it that easy? Just have a bit of success and all doubt goes away?"

"No, not just a bit. It takes a lifetime of success to overcome uncertainty. People are born insecure. It has to be weaned out of us as we grow. Realizing we have talents as children, making friends, accomplishing challenging feats... it all adds up to build a foundation that we can build the remainder of our lives on. That's what happened to so many of the monsters we chase; they failed to build confidence. Actually, most were probably humiliated and dehumanized as children. Combine that with the right strand of DNA, and you have the perfect cocktail for evil."

Captain Johnson burst through the door and pointed to his office.

"See, he isn't happy. Let's go," John said.

"I'm right behind you."

They entered the office and sat across from the captain.

"Well, how'd that go?" John asked.

"Fucking assholes, all of them. The conservatives want more patrol, more boots on the ground. They ask if it's an Islamic terrorist. The liberals want to know if race is involved and if more stringent gun control would solve these abductions. None of them want to get it right, they just want to be right to win the argument. What a way to enter my golden period."

"Golden period?" Ricky echoed.

John looked at the captain with a half-grin and said, "It's the time of your life when you're still physically active and competent and your mental focus is still intact, when all of your experiences and edification has made you wise, much wiser than you were in your unharnessed youth."

"Ah, I see, right before you walk around in an adult diaper, drooling through your dentures," Ricky said.

"Enough of this talk, rookie. Fill me in on what you found out."

"We went by his place, a charming little abode. I then visited his daughter, Alexis. She gave me information on where he hangs to drink his gloom away. The bartender gave us a description of our guy. It's in the report." Ricky said.

"Okay, good. Did the daughter give you anything else?"

"Other than a big hug to lover-boy here, no," John replied.

The captain looked at Ricky. "Keep it in your pants, Romeo, at least until we save her father."

"I'll have the feds do a sketch from the description. Let's see what they come up with. All we can do now is wait for this rat to reach out to us again."

"What if he doesn't?" Ricky asked softly.

John grunted. "He will. That's his vice; the competition of intellects, his and ours. That's what gives him his high."

"I'll give this bastard a high. A 9mm from my Glock between his eyes," Ricky said.

12:58:03, 12:58:02, 12:58:01...

Ricky sat at his desk reviewing files when he received a call on his cell phone from an unknown number.

"Hello?"

"Detective Burton? This is Alexis Carson."

"Hi, Alexis. Is everything okay?"

"Yes, I just wanted to let you know that I talked to my mother and she came clean on my father. He's a veteran. She knew, but never told me."

"Why?"

"He had issues. She wanted to protect me from him. He started drinking heavily and she said he was unstable at times. He never left us, she threw him out when I was very young."

"I'm sorry, Alexis."

"She even changed my last name from his to hers. She told me after she threw him out he lost all control, lost his job, and lived off his welfare check which he would drink away. In reality, he lived off his veterans check. I hated him for leaving me, and all this time it was a lie. May I come in? Maybe I can be of some help to you. I don't want him to die. I need to see him again."

Ricky closed his eyes and ignored every instinct he had. "Sure, you can come in. We're trying to figure out where he's being held. Is there anything else you can tell me that may help us? Anything else your mother said?"

"No. Why, Ricky? Why did he take my father?"

"We don't know. That sad truth is, it may just be a coincidence... wrong place, wrong time."

"That's hard to accept."

"I know, but it may be the only answer."

She sighed. "Okay. I'm leaving now."

"Okay, see you soon."

12:14:03, 12:14:02, 12:14:01...

As Ricky looked up and noticed Alexis Carson walk into the station, he felt an unfamiliar feeling in his stomach. The feeling wasn't exactly butterflies; it was more a rush of excitement akin to how a child would feel on Christmas morning when they first open their eyes, knowing magic awaits them. *What the hell is going on with me?* he thought as he watched a wide smile spread across Alexis' face as she recognized him and started walking toward him. She had on a tight pair of jeans which hugged her curves, a soft white sweater, and her chestnut hair cascading down in layered ringlets.

"Hi," Ricky said as she reached his desk. "Have a seat."

"Thank you. Any new info?"

"Not yet," Ricky said, then cleared his throat. "Alexis, I need to tell you something. This criminal we are dealing with is playing a game with us. He sends us a clue that pertains to the whereabouts of his captive." He paused to gauge how she was taking his words. "I want to be honest with you — he has every intention of killing him. The fate of your father lies in our hands."

Ricky watched her as her eyes dropped, but quickly regained the strength to raise them up and meet his.

"I understand."

"We... have a live video of him back in the captain's office. I shouldn't have told you that, but I can't keep it from you."

"Can I see him?"

"Alexis..."

"Please, I know the situation. I just need to see him."

Ricky ran his hand through his hair, sighed deeply, and stood up. "Okay, follow me."

Ricky saw the captain glance up as he led Alexis into his office. He was talking with the feds, and Ricky knew he wouldn't like the idea of showing Alexis the crime scene with her father captive in what may become a vat of boiling water.

"Have a seat, I'll bring up the video feed. Before I do, I want to warn you that it will be extremely disturbing. Are you sure you want see this?"

"Yes."

Ricky clicked on the feed and the video came to life on the screen. Brian Simmons' body stood limp, held up by the chains attached to his wrists. His complexion had become very pale, almost as if Mr. Simmons' ghost had already taken the place of his body. Viewing his state, Ricky wasn't sure he would live to be boiled alive.

Alexis raised a hand to her mouth in horror. "Oh, *God*. Ricky, what the hell is he going to do with him?"

"We aren't sure," Ricky lied. "We have every intention of solving his riddle and saving your father."

"Riddle?"

"Yes, at twelve hours he sends us a riddle that will aid us in uncovering his whereabouts. Actually, we should be receiving one in about ten minutes." He pointed to the digital clock ticking down in the corner of the screen.

"Why would he do that?"

"It's a game to him. Our intellect against his. Many sociopaths, and, or psychopaths, like to wield their intelligence by creating a competition with the ones attempting to catch them. Our man seems to have a special place in his heart for John, my partner."

Alexis looked away from the screen. "I've seen enough. Thank you"

Ricky gave her a comforting smile. "I'm meeting with John and Captain Johnson in five minutes. You can stay at my desk or in the lunchroom, if you'd like. There's coffee and maybe a few donuts left."

"Okay, I could use a hot coffee."

"Follow me."

12:00:03, 12:00:02, 12:00:01...

The trio gathered around the computer awaiting the clue to arrive on the screen. Suddenly, right on time, it appeared:

MERRY DALE LANE

Merry Dale lane appeared in large, capitalized block letters in Times New Roman text, typed in a violet hue.

"Merry Dale Lane. Anyone heard of it? John?" Captain Johnson asked.

"No. I know this city inside and out. I don't believe there is a Merry Dale Lane."

Captain Johnson picked up his phone. "Marty, run a statewide search for a Merry Dale Lane. Let me know as soon as you're done."

"Why would he send us right to the street? It doesn't make sense. There has to be more to it than that," Ricky said.

Captain Johnson shrugged. "You're probably correct, but let's start with the most obvious then work our way from there."

John continued to stare at the text on the bottom of the screen. Brian Simmons started pulling against his restraints and shaking uncontrollably. John's eyes landed on the poor man submerged in water up to his shoulders.

"Even if we're able to find this poor guy, he'll be totally insane by then. Look at him."

His two colleagues joined him as they watched Brian Simmons finally relax and slouch back down, having depleted his body of its final energy supply.

"Captain, pick up," Marty Burns said over the intercom.

"What do you got for me, Marty?" The captain paused, then: "Nothing? Okay, expand to neighboring states... Idaho, Montana, Oregon, just to be sure."

"He is in Washington, he wouldn't leave the state. He wants a fair competition. It is his code, just like there is a code here in this text somehow," John said.

"Well, let's figure it out," Ricky replied.

11:45:03, 11:45:02, 11:45:01...

Ricky entered the lunchroom, sat down across from Alexis and smiled. As she smiled back, he once again felt his stomach flutter. Her smile was a drug to him, and he was quickly becoming addicted.

"Hi, did you eat? There's some food in the fridge."

"No, thank you, coffee is enough," she said as she gripped the steaming cup in front of her.

'Alexis, does Merry Dale Lane mean anything to you?"

"No, why would it?"

"He sent it to us, as a clue. I'm just being thorough."

"He really pisses me off. My father's life is at stake, and he's making a game out of it."

"I know, but that's the point. It's him versus us; only the best wins."

"Yeah, but he has the deck slanted in his favor."

"Of course he does, but it's the only game he's willing to play and if we want a chance to save your father, we need to follow his rules."

Alexis looked down into her cup and a pang shot through Ricky's heart. He put his hand over hers.

"Look at me. I will do everything I can to save him. We'll figure this thing out."

"Promise me."

Ricky looked away for an instant and decided to give an answer that he prayed he would not regret.

"I promise. I promise you will see your father alive again."

11:00:03, 11:00:02, 11:00:01...

"There is no Merry Dale Lane on the West Coast. In fact, the closest Merry Dale Lane is on the East Coast in South Carolina and Georgia," Captain Johnson said.

"Okay, so what else could it mean? It is definitely an address, encoded somehow," John replied.

"Expand our search to addresses that include Merry, Dale, and Lane separately. Maybe something will hit that makes sense," Ricky said.

"Does anyone else think the color of the text means something? Captain? Ricky? The text he sent for the Kerry Reid case was all black, along with his greeting. Now he switched to purple."

"Purple, what the hell could that mean?" Ricky said.

"We need to expand our searches to every city, town, street, avenue, and lane that includes purple in its name," Captain Johnson said as he hurried out of his office to track down officer Burns.

John noticed Ricky glance at him, a small frown on his lips and his eyes blinking repeatedly. John knew something wasn't right with his young colleague.

"Ricky, what is it? Do you have an idea what this means?"

Ricky ran his hand through his short dark hair and lowered his head.

"Seriously, what the hell is it? You look like you are about ready to puke," John said.

"John, I fucked up. I promised Alexis we'd find him, alive and well. What if we can't? Something about this woman makes me do things I know I shouldn't. Things that go against my training, decisions made against my better judgment. I feel like I have no control when I'm with her."

"Seems to me like you're falling for her, rookie. You need to separate emotion from the equation. I know it's difficult, but every decision we make, everything we do, is decided by analytical thinking unless my instinct tells me differently," John said. "You'll be fine, Ricky. Just think before you make promises you aren't sure you can keep. We will find him, don't worry."

"What if we don't?"

"Well, if we don't there is always online dating."

10:22:03, 10:22:02, 10:22:01...

The dark figure watched as his captive slumped, his weight being held up only by his restraints. He turned the sound up on his computer and adjusted the screen to its brightest setting. Night had crept in, turning the video feed gloomy and shadowy. He knew his prey had given up hope and welcomed death. Thoughts circled his mind: *This is the high I crave, the ability to play God, to decide who lives or dies, just because I have the power to. This is what my life has become, this is what I have become, and I love myself for it. There are no demons, there are no voices. I kill because I enjoy it and it is a means to an end. I have found my reason for being here, my higher calling... and I couldn't be happier.*

9:43:03, 9:43:02, 9:43:01...

John leaned back in his chair and interlocked his hands behind his head in a gesture infused with stress. As his eyes wandered from the ceiling back down to his desk, they came to rest on a picture of his family he recently placed next to his computer. It was the family enjoying Easter dinner together a few years back, taken by Julie's mother. John sat at the head of the table smiling happily with a prideful glow. Julie was wearing a white sundress, looking like an angel sent from above. Ryann sported khaki pants and a white button-down shirt, one of the few times he would be caught in formal clothes. Then his sight came to rest on his baby girl. She wore a purple sundress, a smile from ear to ear and a bright, brilliant glow overtaking her face. *She is such a beautiful girl, on her way to becoming a woman,* he thought. Then a memory shot into his mind. A conversation they had that day while eating dinner came back to him like it was yesterday...

"Gianna, I like your purple dress," Ryann said.
"Yes, it's very pretty, darling," Julie chimed in.

"Thank you, but it's not purple," Gianna replied.
"Looks purple to me," Ryann said.
"It's lavender, you fool."

John sat up like he was shot out of a rocket, jumped to his feet and rushed into the captain's office. He brought the address back onto the screen:

MERRY DALE LANE

Why, you mother fucker. John picked up the phone and called the captain and Ricky, who were in the office with the feds. "Guys, get in here quick."

Moments later the duo rushed into the room.

"What is it?" Ricky said.

"Occam's Razor," John answered.

"What? Okum's what?" The captain asked.

"Occam's Razor, I know it. It's a scientific philosophy written by William Ockham, an English friar and theologian. It means the simplest solution is usually the correct solution," Ricky said.

"Exactly," John replied.

"Well I'll be damned, I didn't know I was dealing with two Rhodes Scholars," the captain said. "But, just what the hell does that have to do with our little clue."

"The text is lavender, not purple. What town do we know that is famous for lavender? What town is actually the lavender capital of the world?"

"Holy shit... Sequim."

John nodded his head and said, "Gentlemen, Brain Simmons is being held somewhere in Sequim."

9:23:03, 9:23:02, 9:23:01...

Marty entered the office responding to the captain's request.

"Marty, jot this down. I want a search of Sequim, Washington. Search for any street, lane, boulevard, road, drive, or highway that may include the words merry and/or dale. Please be quick, we have just over nine hours to save this man," the captain said as he pointed to the screen.

"Yes, of course, sir."

As John watched Marty Burns rush out a feeling of nausea came over him. He walked out of the office and through the front door of the station to get some air. He bent over and put his hands on his knees as he took a couple of deep breaths. Slowly, his queasiness faded. As he stood up and looked up at the sun which was partially tucked behind a white fluffy cloud, he thought: *This world can be so beautiful, so clean. Why must it be inhabited by evil, sick people who only want to destroy innocence and good?* He looked around at the people living their lives, the mailman delivering a love letter to a woman who had long ago given up hope, an old man walking his dog with gentleness and love, a young woman holding her toddler's hand with pride as she leads him into the barbershop for a haircut.

So much love is around us, everywhere. Why can't we keep the innocent safe? Why must there be unrelenting evil? After thirty years I still ask the same questions. When will it end? When will I stop seeing innocent faces being torn apart in my dreams. John quickly walked over to the side of the building, bent down, and vomited in the grass.

8:22:03, 8:2202, 8:22:01...

John washed up in the bathroom and walked back into the office.

"Hey, where've you been? There were no matches for merry or dale in Sequim," Ricky said.

"Where's the captain?"

"He's with Marty, researching the roads of Sequim. John, do you have any ideas? I keep looking at the text, but nothing comes to me. Alexis asked me if we are making any progress and I don't know how to answer. I told her we narrowed it down to one town, Sequim. She looked like she had no idea where that is. John? Jesus, you look terrible, pallid. Are you okay?"

"Pallid? What the hell is that?"

"Pale, white," Ricky said impatiently. "Like you just saw a ghost."

John's ears went deaf after the last sentence came out of Ricky's mouth. He was staring at the screen with an intense look in his eyes.

"John? What is it?"

Ricky, jot these words down."

Ricky pulled out his pad and pen and looked up at John.

"Happy, Cheer, glee, joy, sunny, vale, valley, ravine, glade, dell."

"Got it. Any more?"

"Let's start there," John replied.

"Wait, I don't understand—"

"Synonyms Ricky, they are synonyms of the words he gave us."

Ricky jumped up after nearly falling off the chair and ran out of the office to find the captain, John assumed. A small smile came over his lips as he glanced at Brian Simmons. *Hang in there, sir. We are coming.*

7:58:03, 7:58:02, 7:58:01…

"There's a Happy Valley Road in Sequim. I'm sending all the available men I have to search for any shed, hut, shack, shanty, or outhouse." Captain Johnson pointed to locations on a digital map on his computer. "The feds will start from the east, here, where it meets 101. Our men will start from the west, here, where it meets River Road,"

"That road must be ten miles long, it's going to take some time to cover that ground," Ricky said.

"That's why we're going to get out there to help. Captain, as soon as you coordinate the search, let us know," John said.

"I'll let you know as soon as I map it out. It will take you an hour to an hour and a half even with your lights and sirens active, so hit the road ASAP. I'll be directing search groups on the fly."

"Will do. Ricky, meet me at my truck in ten."

"You got it." Ricky rushed out of the office and headed for the lunchroom. He saw Alexis, stretched out on the couch in the small rec room off the back of the lunchroom. He walked over and knelt beside her, brushed her hair out of her face and waited for her to stir. Her eyes slowly opened, and a small smile appeared.

"Hi," she said as she sat up.

"Hi, I'm sorry for waking you but I wanted to fill you in on the case. We think we have the street. We are all heading there for the search in ten minutes."

"Where?" she replied as her eyes grew wide in wonder.

"Happy Valley Road in Sequim. It's a few hours west of Seattle."

"Are you sure?"

"We're fairly certain. We'll find him, Alexis, or die trying."

6:42:03, 6:42:02, 6:42:01...

John turned west onto Happy Valley Road with Ricky by his side.

"Captain wants us to search between Sporseen Road and McFarland Drive, on the western section of Happy Valley."

"Got it. I think I know the area," John replied.

As John drove west they saw many officers from the Sequim Police department already searching their assigned areas for every shed, shack or hut they could find. John felt that with just under seven hours to spare, they would find Mr. Simmons. Hopefully, alive.

"We'll get to him, Ricky," John said as he turned and nodded to his partner.

Ricky nodded back and let out a deep sigh as they continued west towards their destination.

6:32:03, 6:32:02, 6:32:01...

They arrived at their location, parked, and exited the truck.

"You take the north side and I'll take the south side. We'll start at McFarland Drive and work our way west to Sporseen," John said.

"Sounds good," Ricky said. "Good luck."

John watched him cross the road and they both started their trek on opposite sides. John searched a small wooded area directly off the road where McFarland Drive meets Happy Valley Road. He cleared the grove and entered what looked to be a small industrial building with a couple of steel storage facilities.

"Can I help you?" a man in overalls said as he walked towards John.

"Hi, my name is Detective Corbin," John said as he held up his badge. "Not sure if you have noticed the police activity on Happy Valley Road, but we're searching for a missing person and believe him to be in the area. May I take a quick look around?"

"Sure, anything to help, detective."

"Thank you." John cleared the two buildings and retreated west down Happy Valley Road as he gave a courtesy wave to the worker. The South side of the road contained thick woods with few buildings. He would have to clear the woods up to Sporseen Road, as deep as he could. John took a deep breath, glanced at the bright, blue Sequim sky's descending sun, and entered the trees.

6:28:03, 6:28:02, 6:28:01...

Ricky approached a large, residential house and knocked on the door. He would have to clear as much as he could without a search warrant, hopefully with the consent of the resident. But, with someone's life being at stake, he was prepared to do what he had to. He would make sure Brian Simmons wasn't being held anywhere on the land he was responsible for.

The door opened and an attractive woman in her thirties opened with a small child grasping her leg. Ricky already had his badge out at eye level.

"May I help you, officer?"

"Yes, ma'am. We have reason to believe a missing person is being held in this area. I would like your permission to search and clear this house and land. You will be doing everyone involved in the search effort a great service and may help us save a life."

The woman focused on Ricky's eyes, looked down at his gun and two- way radio before cracking a slight smile and agreeing.

"Thank you, Ma'am. It will only take a minute or two."

"I noticed the heavy presence of police in the area. I hope you find him or her."

"Him, and thanks again."

After clearing the area, Ricky said goodbye and continued down the northern side through a small wooded lot. When he reached the end of his designated area and found nothing of significance, he radioed John. "Nothing here, over."

"10-4. Same on my end. Meet me back at the truck," John answered. Just as John broke the tree line and quickened his pace towards his vehicle, he noticed Ricky cross the street from the opposite side. They met at the truck and got in. John radioed Captain Johnson to brief him.

"Sir, we got nothing."

"John, I have great news, they just found him. He was being held in a wooden shed just east of Happy Valley Alpaca Ranch, behind a small pond in a thicket of trees."

"I'm heading there now," John said as he turned the truck around and raced east to the site.

6:21:03, 6:21:02, 6:21:01…

John pulled his truck over at the rear of a collection of assorted cruisers, unmarked federal agent cars and SUVs, a Sequim fire truck, and ambulance. The shed was located between the ranch and Osprey Gun Road, a thousand feet south off Happy Valley Road. John jumped out of the truck with Ricky following close behind and headed for the congregation of officers and agents on the side of the road.

"Hi, I'm Detective Corbin and this is my partner, Detective Burton from the Seattle force."

An agent nodded to them. "Hello, detectives. The victim was being held in a secluded shed approximately a thousand feet south behind a small pond." The federal agent pointed passed an open field into a thicket of trees.

"Thank you." John and Ricky rushed across the field to the area of where their man had been found. As they approached, the small pond came into view and they saw officers grouped around their destination. They reached the woods and immediately saw the shanty, surrounded by the authorities with the door open. John rushed to the doorway and peered in. Mr. Simmons was being released from his bindings as John entered. They had shot out the glass and the water had rushed over the floor and found its path to the dry earth below.

"My God," Ricky breathed as he followed John into the structure. "He looks like he's already dead."

"No, he'll be fine. He's dehydrated and exhausted. They'll take care of him," John said.

The paramedics placed him on a stretcher and wheeled him out. "Get him into the ambulance. I want an IV hooked up STAT. We need to get fluids and nutrients into his bloodstream as quickly as possible," the lead medic said as Ricky followed them out of the woods toward the ambulance.

John watched them wheel Brian Simmons away on the stretcher, alive and soon to be on the road to recovery. He looked around the small enclosure, which was Mr. Simmons own personal cell for almost eighteen hours. He noticed the shattered glass from the vat the captive was to be boiled in scattered all over the shed's floor. He looked up at the wall and located a small camera, the camera the sick and twisted murderer used to watch his prey plead for his life. John Corbin looked directly into the camera as a wide grin appeared on his mouth. He then mouthed the words "FUCK YOU" as he lifted his middle finger up and held it there, making sure the evil psychopath on the other end wouldn't miss it.

The dark figure watched the process as it played out. He saw them break into the shed, shoot out the glass, and witnessed the water flow out of the tank as an anger started to rise inside him. He didn't like to lose. He didn't like to be outsmarted by the authorities, least of all John Corbin. He threw his drink against the wall and the glass shattered much like the receptacle which held his quarry. As he looked back at the screen, he saw them lead his prey away to safety, followed by a familiar face. He watched closely as John Corbin smirked at him, told him to go fuck himself, and then unbelievingly, he gave him the finger. The dark figure got up and threw his desk over, sending his computer screen crashing to the floor in a heap.

"*NOOOOOOOOOO!*" he screamed as he walked out, knowing he was beaten at his own game by the one man he so desperately wanted to destroy.

Detective John Corbin.

CHAPTER FIVE

While making his way back to Seattle, Ricky phoned Alexis to inform her that her father was safe.

"Hello?"

"I have good news, we found him. He's on his way to the hospital now."

"Oh my, thank you, Ricky! What hospital? When can I go see him?"

"He's heading to the Harbor View Hospital, but please wait the night. He's in rough shape and needs medical care and rest. I'll take you tomorrow. I have to go now, but I wanted to let you know he's going to be fine."

"Ricky, thank you. I trusted you and you didn't let me down. I won't ever forget that."

"No need to thank me. It's my job and I'm happy to help. Goodnight, get some rest."

"I will, goodnight."

Ricky walked into Harbor View Hospital shortly after the ambulance containing Brian Simmons arrived. He approached the front desk as a middle-aged man in scrubs looked up with welcoming eyes.

Ricky showed his badge. "Hi, my name is Detective Burton and I'd like to visit the room of Brian Simmons, the man picked up from Sequim two hours ago."

The man in scrubs looked at the badge with an experienced eye. "Good evening, detective." He then went to his chart. "Let me look up Mr. Simmons for you. I saw them wheel him in." He paused a moment, then said, "Seems he's doing very well. He's in room 313. The elevator is right around the corner," the man said as he pointed down the hallway to the left.

"Thank you."

Ricky entered the elevator and pushed the button to the third floor. Before the doors closed, a young, attractive female doctor walked in, smiled at him, and pushed the second-floor button. It never ceased to amaze Ricky how lives are a combination of luck, timing, and decisions. Mr. Simmons, upstairs in a hospital bed, was lucky to be alive. For himself, lucky to be in an elevator with a beautiful doctor whom he would have interest in, *if* he hadn't met Mr. Simmons incredible daughter because of some psycho kidnapped him. Fate. The twists and turns of all lives can change on a dime, without reason, without control, without a definite destiny. The elevator doors opened on the second floor and the attractive doctor walked out of Ricky's life, probably never to enter it again.

Ricky exited the elevator on the third floor and walked to room 313. The door was closed with a pair of doctors discussing their new patient in the hallway. When Ricky stopped, they both looked up.

Ricky again pulled his badge. "Good evening, gentlemen, I'm Detective Burton. I would like to ask Mr. Simmons a few questions, if he's up to it."

The doctor on the right looked at his partner, who Ricky assumed was the ranked doctor on this case.

The doctor on the left spoke. "Hello, detective. I'm Doctor Bradford and this is my colleague, Doctor Wentz. Mr. Simmons is doing fine. We're giving him fluids and nutrients intravenously. He was dehydrated and weak, however, it doesn't seem he's at risk of having any lasting effects... physical effects, anyway."

"That's great news. Is he coherent? Can he speak?"

"Sure, go on in. Please limit your visit to fifteen minutes, though. He needs his rest."

"Thank you."

Ricky entered the room and sat in the chair beside the bed. Brian Simmons opened his eyes and Ricky couldn't help but notice the same sea-green eyes that his daughter possessed.

"Hello, Mr. Simmons. My name is Detective Burton and I was part of the task force that rescued you."

"Thank you," he replied with a bit of effort.

"No need to thank me, I'm just glad we were able to find you." Ricky pulled out his small note book. "Now, is there anything you can tell me? Do you remember your abductor? Do you remember where or when he took you?"

"Nope, all I remember is walking out of the bar and heading home. Next thing I know, I woke up in that trap. I felt like I was back in Nam. They would torture us that way, string us up and beat us. Threaten us with all different sorts of punishments."

"I'm sorry you had to go through that, sir. It must have been horrible."

"I never even saw him. I'm sorry, I can't help you there."

"I understand. Mr. Simmons, do you have any enemies? Anyone who would have a purpose or reason to do this?"

"Hmm, just my ex-wife," he replied with a chuckle.

Ricky smiled. "Well, I think we can rule her out at this point. There *is* something I need to tell you that may come as a bit of a shock. I've been in contact with your daughter. She knows what happened." Ricky noticed the immediate reaction from the older man. Mr. Simmons eyes lit up like a candle.

"Alexis? How...?"

"We found her. I went to her apartment for information. She's fine. She knows you are safe."

"Thank you, detective...Barton?"

"Burton, but you can call me Ricky."

"Thank you, Ricky. That means the world to me."

Ricky closed his notepad and pocketed it. "I'm going to let you get some sleep. I'll check in tomorrow. Sometimes it takes a day or two for certain memories to return. We can try again after you've rested. Goodnight, sir."

As Ricky walked to the door and opened it to leave, Mr. Simmons called out, "Ricky, does she want to see me?"

"Well, we'll see what we can do. Something tells me she may be by to see you tomorrow." Ricky gave Mr. Simmons a wide smile then turned and walked out.

John entered the station and walked into Captain Johnson's office. The captain stood, and the two comrades shook hands without saying a word before they both sat down.

"*This*. This is the reason I'm still involved, John. The feeling you get when you save someone. The rush of euphoria you feel from extending a life as a result of your hard work. I know I don't have to explain that to you."

John nodded, smiled and said, "Great work, Michael. There's no better feeling in the world."

"Tonight, we celebrate my friend. I'll call Sarah and inform her I won't be home for dinner. Let's hit the tavern for drinks."

"Sure, Red is on the bar tonight. He'll be happy to see us."

"Perfect. Where's Ricky?"

"He went to the hospital to check on Mr. Simmons."

"Okay, inform him of our plans."

"Of course. I'm heading home to check in with the wife and kids. I'll see you in a bit," After John left, the captain leaned back in his chair with his hands behind his head, a feeling of conquest and triumph engulfing him.

***

Ricky knocked lightly on Alexis' door. He needed to see her. Partly to tell her about her father, but also just because he missed her. She opened the door and immediately jumped into his arms.

"Oh, Ricky, thank you!" she said as she hugged him and kissed his cheek. Ricky felt an intense twinge from his groin as he felt her lips against his cheek and detected her sweet vanilla scent from her skin and hair.

"You are very welcome," he said, catching her in his surprise. "John just informed me we're celebrating at his restaurant. I'd love for you to join me, after I fill you in on your dad, of course."

"Oh, I'd love to accompany you. Come in and have a seat, I just need to finish this paragraph." Alexis led Ricky to the couch.

"What are you writing?"

"My third book, I'm an author."

"What kind of books do you write?"

"Romance. Are you a romantic, Detective Burton?"

"I read mostly non-fiction, but I can make an exception."

"Okay, here." Alexis handed him a book with a couple of lovers kissing on the cover titled, *The Secret Desire*.

Ricky sat down, thumbing through the book. "Thank you, I look forward to reading it." He changed the subject to something a bit more serious. "He's doing well. He doesn't remember anything about his abductor, but it may take a bit of time for certain details to come back to him. They're giving him fluids and nutrients and he needs his rest, but I think tomorrow you should go to see him."

"It may be a bit overwhelming. Will you come with me?"

"Of course I will," Ricky answered with a smile. "Now I'm going to shower, I'll be back in an hour to pick you up, if that works for you."

Alexis walked Ricky to the door and as he turned to say goodbye, she slowly and softly touched her lips to his and let them linger for a bit. He tasted her natural essence as her lips opened and closed in a gentle kiss. She smiled as she shut the door behind him. As he walked to his car, he was so dizzy from her touch he almost lost his footing.

***

It was a packed night at the tavern. John sat at the bar between Captain Johnson and Ricky, who was flanked by Alexis. Sean, Artie, and Matt were also present as Red worked the bar.

"Red, grab a free round for the bar on me," John said which instantly obtained the attention of Sean who had just finished off his beer.

"I think I'm in love," Sean said as he waved in an appreciative gesture to John.

"New woman in your life, Sean? I thought you were married?" Matt said.

"Not a woman, dude. Any dude that buys me a beer has earned my affection."

Artie gave a quick chuckle as Red made his way to their end of the bar to take their drink orders.

"Another Brooklyn, Sean? Another Sangria, Artie?"

"You got it, boss," Sean said.

"Yup, another Sangria will hit the spot," Artie replied.

"Matt?" As Red looked up he noticed Matt's attention had waned. He looked to see what had caught Matt's eye. A teenage girl was making her way back from the ladies room to her parent's table.

"Matt!" Red said which jolted Matt from his daydream. "What the heck are you looking at? You could be her father."

"What? No, wait, I wasn't. That's not what I was looking at. I went to Brown!"

Red looked at him disapprovingly. "What do you want to drink, you pervert."

Matt's eyes drooped in embarrassment. "A Brown University."

Red shook his head and walked away to make their drinks. At the other end of the bar the drinks were flowing and the party was just getting started. Sarah, the captain's wife, joined them as well as Marty and a few of the federal agents. They all ate and celebrated their well-deserved victory; a victory not only over one lunatic, but over evil in general — an evil that takes innocent lives, inflicts pain on the least deserving and fractures families and obliterates the love they feel. As

John looked around the bar at his comrades, his friends, he thought to himself, *This is why I returned. This is why I do this. Nothing else can make me feel this way.*

At the end of the night, Red drove John home and as John got out, he thanked his partner and headed inside. He petted Simba, who had run downstairs to greet him and made his way upstairs. He entered Ryann's room and walked over and kissed his son on the forehead, careful not to wake him. Next, he walked into Gianna's room and sat down on the bed beside her. His daughter opened her eyes and said, "Hi, Daddy. I couldn't sleep until you got home. Sometimes I worry about you out there, chasing criminals."

"I know, sweetheart. I'm very careful. We had a very good night," he said with a wide smile.

"That's good, did you catch the bad guy?"

"Well, no, not yet. But, we saved an innocent man who didn't deserve to die, which is even better. Go to sleep now, princess. I love you."

"I love you too, daddy."

John left her room and walked into his bedroom, crawled into bed and put his arm around Julie. Simba jumped on the bed and chose a spot by John's feet. John slept through the night without interruption. For the first night in a while, no nightmares came.

Ricky escorted Alexis to the hospital the following day just as he said he would. They approached room 313 and walked in together. Ricky noticed the spark in Mr. Simmons' eyes as he watched his daughter walk over to the side of his bed.

"Hello Mr. Simmons. I brought someone here who wants to talk to you." Ricky stepped out of the room to give Alexis and her father some privacy.

Alexis reached down and took hold of her dad's hand.

"Alexis, I want you to know I never wanted to leave you, but I had to for reasons I can't explain."

"Would those reasons happen to include my mother throwing you out?" Alexis asked.

He looked away, ashamed of what had become of their family, remorseful for the kind of father he was to Alexis.

"She told me everything. I made her. I understand you had issues that required some help, but I also understand it wasn't your choice. I finally know who you really are and what you've been through. Daddy, I forgive you."

As he took in his daughter's words a tear fell from his eye and a smile appeared.

"Thank you, Alexis. You have no idea what that means to me."

"I'm going to get you help as soon as you can leave here. We'll work together to get you well, quit drinking, make sure you eat healthily, and find a decent place for you to live."

"You don't need to do all that. I'm fine where I am. I eat okay. Sure, I need to give up the drink, but I get by."

"You get by, but you don't live. I'm going to help you live again, so save your protests."

He looked his daughter in the eyes and sighed. "I can see you've inherited your mother's stubbornness."

Alexis smiled and reached down to give her father a hug while Ricky watched through the doorway, happy he helped reunite them.

December 13, 2003...

John took the week off and planned a skiing trip to Stevens Pass Mountain Resort. He picked Julie up on Saturday and they drove up to Skykomish. John had recently been promoted to detective and Julie, after years of schooling, had recently progressed from a CNA to a surgical nurse. This trip was exactly what the couple needed: a quiet place where they could spend quality time together and celebrate their accomplishments. On the drive up, John looked over to Julie and said, "It's been a wonderful four years together, sweetie."

"I've enjoyed every minute of it," Julie replied with a smile. That smile. Nothing could brighten John's world like it. He thought how lucky he was on that cold December night four years ago when their paths crossed. He was either blessed, lucky... or maybe a combination of both.

The couple checked into the resort and spent the week together, enjoying each day more than the last. On the final day after skiing and dinner, they retired to their suite where a roaring fire blazed in the fireplace and a bottle of red wine awaited. John proposed in front of the flames and they made love countless times, celebrating the life they planned to share together. That night, between the throws of passion and love, a seed was planted; a seed that would become Gianna Corbin, their first child.

Ricky stood outside the room with his back against the wall and his .40 caliber pulled out and ready. He heard a baby wailing, checked the countdown on his watch... 12, 11, 10... then after he heard what sounded like a saw turn on, he kicked the door in. In front of him, strapped to a conveyer belt is an infant, maybe six months old. The belt was connected to a table saw and the infant was moving toward it. Four feet, three feet, two feet. Ricky froze, and that lost time cost the baby its life as the saw splits it in two from head to toe. Blood sprayed everywhere as the weeping subsided and Ricky collapsed onto the floor, covered in innocent blood. The tears came and Ricky put the pistol to his temple and pulled the trigger...

He sat up in a terrified panic as the sweat poured off his face and down his neck. He was overtaken with relief as reality came back to him, and he realized it was only a nightmare. He pulled the covers aside, crawled out of bed and headed to the bathroom to urinate and splash cold water on his face. The memory of the night's activities returned: the party at John's restaurant, the drinks, taking Alexis home and kissing her goodnight. How he wanted to take her to bed, but he knew it wasn't the right time. She was much different than all the others. He wanted to build something special, something that would last.

After dousing his face, Ricky stood in front of the mirror, looked at his reflection and searched for answers. Why have the nightmares increased in abundance and intensity? Will they ever subside? Will he ever sleep peacefully again? The images of the nightmare returned to his mind... so vivid, so real.

He stumbled into bed and clicked the television on. He found an old movie that comforted him when he was a child, so he dropped the remote on the bed. No sleep came.

John took the following few days off, the first to recover from the celebration, and the second to spend the day with his family. He took them to the Seattle Museum of Pop Culture, a place Gianna had wanted to experience for a few years now. The children had a blast visiting the fantasy, horror, and video game exhibits in the morning and the family was famished by lunchtime. They decided to get some burgers and fries at an outside stand and took the food to a picnic table. When finished, John took the litter to a garbage bin and as he dumped the wrappers, used napkins, and paper cups into the trash, something caught his eye. A fly was trapped in a plastic bag that had melted cheese in it. The opening to the bag was folded over so the fly's only way out was blocked. John watched as the fly panicked, furiously searching for a break in the plastic. It was an anxious hysteria all too common in John's world. The victim, realizing he or she is caught in a trap, likely to never escape is first confused, then panics, and finally the morbid acceptance of their destiny is realized, cumulating in probable death; the point at which that the prey knows he or she will never see their loved ones again, never smile again, or eat their favorite food. Never hear their favorite song or watch their favorite movie for the hundredth time.

"John, are you okay?" Julie asked as she walked over without John even hearing her footsteps.

"Sure," he said as he reached into the bin and flipped the bag over, releasing the fly from its prison. It flew away, its wings fluttering frantically, and John wondered if the insect knew how lucky it really was to be free.

The following day the team met back at the station. Everyone was in a significantly better mood and frame of mind since the last time they were here all together. John, Ricky, and Captain Johnson were all present when Marty walked in with a scowl on his face.

"Marty, you look like someone just kicked your dog. What's up?" Captain Johnson asked.

"Nothing, just a bad night. Argued with the wife, didn't sleep, and then this morning I noticed my hair is really thinning out. What the heck's up with that? I'm only thirty-five. I'm too young to go bald."

"Nature is selecting you out of the gene pool," Ricky said.

"What the hell do you mean?"

"Nature pretty much wants you to be fat, bald and unattractive. That way, no female in her right mind would accept your sperm into her body," Ricky said.

"Nature doesn't want your crusty, old sperm reproducing," John said as he winked at Ricky.

"Damn, so nature is telling me it's time to just sit in a rocking chair and grow old?"

John grinned. "Exactly. Grow old and drink ensure until you die, but for fuck's sake, don't spread your ancient seed."

"But you're older than me and you have a full head of hair."

"Yeah, but I'm special... and sexy."

"Wonderful. Thanks a lot, guys."

"Hey, don't thank us, thank nature," Ricky quipped.

"Are you guys going to get any work done, or just bust Marty's balls all day?" Captain Johnson said.

"Definitely bust Marty's balls all day," Ricky said.

"Me too," John added.

The captain closed the file he was holding and said, "Well in that case, I'll join you two. Marty, do you realize you blind me when the sun reflects off your head?"

Everyone joined in the laughter, even Marty.

The dark figure watched the Corbin children as they walked to the bus stop early in the morning. He noticed how the older child, the female, paid close attention to her younger brother. He studied their routine, day after day, noticing every detail.

The devil is in the details, he thought as he watched the school bus pull away. He studied The Corbin's schedule, when they work, when they eat dinner, when they go to bed... all that information settled into his mind and he thought the time to strike was almost here.

Let's see if you give me the finger after this, you son of a bitch, he thought darkly. He drove away with a smug smile on his face. His plan was coming together; a plan that would shake John Corbin's world to the core.

September 23, 2004...

Julie's water broke as she slowly climbed out of the shower. She froze, looked down, and knew it was time. She called John into the bathroom and together they prepared for the trek to the hospital. Thirty-two minutes later, the nurses were propping her up in a bed and getting ready for the delivery. She decided to have a natural childbirth.

"Julie, my dear, this baby is coming soon. You're already at ten centimeters. We have an impatient little baby on our hands," the nurse said.

John held Julie's hand as the doctor entered the room. "I hear we're progressing quickly!" the doctor said.

"Progressing? We're ready," the nurse replied.

A few minutes later, Gianna Rose Corbin entered the world as a healthy, pink, seven pounds, thirteen-ounce baby girl. Julie handled the delivery as well as could be expected without the use of drugs. John cut the umbilical cord and soon after was holding his own flesh and blood. He felt like he was living in his own movie, a movie about his life. It was surreal, wonderful, humbling, uplifting, exhilarating, and an utterly terrifying experience. With all these emotions present, he didn't know exactly what he was feeling. Then, little Gianna looked straight at him and their eyes met for the first time; her eyes, big and brown, and full of life. A few tears fell as he was overwhelmed with an emotion he had never experienced before — the love for your own child.

John and Captain Johnson were going over some paperwork when Ricky eagerly walked up to them.

"I don't understand something. Why? Why does he want to go through these silly tactics? Wouldn't it be much safer if he just killed the people and left them? He's making himself vulnerable continuing these contrivances. It's a paradox. It goes against what he's trying to accomplish."

John looked up at Ricky, quickly glanced at the captain, then back to his younger partner.

"See, that's where you're wrong. You're assuming what he is trying to accomplish. You, a sane and rational man, are trying to decipher what a psychopath is thinking and feeling while looking through your own eyes. It's a lesson learned from the earliest of alienists and followed by criminal profilers. To understand the insane or the psychotic, we must look through their eyes, and their eyes only. He isn't just trying to kill... he wants to win the game. He wants to beat us at his own game, and each step along the way he raises the stakes, culminating in his eventual reason for playing."

"Okay, so for what reason?" Ricky asked.

"That, we won't find out till the end, unless we catch him before then and end the game ourselves," Captain Johnson said.

"Exactly. Your paradox is what makes him tick. He kills to play the game, not vice versa," John said.

"Well, he's a sick, twisted fuck," Ricky said as he exited the office.

The Captain packed up his things and left for the evening.

John headed through the station to go home when Ricky cut him off at his desk.

"Hey, got a sec before you go?"

"Sure, what's up?"

"I wanted to thank you. If it weren't for your insight and instinct, we may not have found him. I wouldn't have known how to face Alexis. You saved him, and you may have saved our relationship."

"Well, first off, you're welcome. Secondly, are we calling this a relationship all ready? You work fast, Romeo."

"I am actually taking things a bit slowly with her. I want this to last and to do that, the foundation has to be solid."

"I couldn't have said it better myself," John said.

"How did you know? I mean, how did it come so easily to you? I thought you were crazy with some of your ideas, but I was wrong."

"Those who dance are considered insane by those who can't hear the music."

"*Nietzsche*," Ricky said.

"You got it. You are an intelligent, driven detective, Ricky. However, sometimes stepping outside of your box, the box of reason, analytics, of rational thought, can help you understand things that you normally wouldn't."

"I understand, and I'm learning. You're a great teacher and mentor."

"Thank you," John answered.

"Oh, I almost forgot, I read your book."

"The Fountainhead?"

"Yes, I liked it. It made me feel rejuvenated and cleansed when I finished it. It kind of rekindled my faith in humanity and what we can accomplish with integrity and desire."

John smiled. "I'm glad you felt that way, I did as well the first time I read it, and every time after."

"How many times have you read it?"

"I'm not sure. I read it every couple of years. In this business, you need to do everything you can to remain sane and pure."

"Hey, do you mind if I let Alexis borrow it? I think she would enjoy it."

"Of course not. How did the reunion go?" John asked.

"I think they're going to have a healthy, long-lasting father-daughter relationship. It couldn't have gone any better."

"I'm happy to hear it. After all, he'll be your father-in-law one day."

Ricky stood up, winked at John, and walked out.

November 1, 2006...

John held his newborn son, Ryann, as a feeling of immense pride came over him. Many of the emotions he felt from this birth were similar to the birth of his daughter two years ago, but some were very different. In both instances, he felt an intense love that he had never experienced before fatherhood. But having a son gave him a strong feeling of pride. He had produced another man to continue the Corbin name. A boy who John would teach to become a man who respects values and women, takes pride in his work, and is faithful to his friends and family. John walked over to the side of the bed and placed his son in Julie's arms. This time, Julie had been in a prolonged labor and she was exhausted. She glanced up at John and smiled before kissing her baby boy on the top of his head and closing her eyes to rest. John imagined what experiences the following years would bring; playing catch in the yard, spending football Sundays together, teaching Ryann how to knot a tie. His mind turned to Gianna who was outside the door in the waiting area with her grandparents and thought: *I now have a family containing everything I have ever wanted.*

The bright sun starting its early morning rise on the eastern horizon as the dark figure stepped out into a warm breeze coming off Elliot Bay. He raised his head to take in the scent of the ocean and feel the sun's rays on his face. *Today is the day,* he thought as his mind focused on his plan. Good timing and flawless, efficient execution were what he needed to make this day a success. He checked his watch and locked his door. *You can never be too careful,* he thought. *There are many dishonest criminals around the city of Seattle.* He double checked the door to make sure it was secure, then headed to his SUV, entered and drove away, looking forward to the task ahead.

He arrived at his destination early, as he was always punctual. Nothing irritated him more than someone being late for an appointment, as it showed a lack of respect for others. He sat back and meditated for a bit while he waited for his prey to arrive. He knew there would be a short window of time when the target would be alone. He had watched this day unfold many times, noticing the movements, scouting the timing of the actions.

"Efficient execution," he whispered to himself as he patiently awaited his chance to strike. The time had come. There, up ahead, his prey had become visible. He exited his vehicle and paused.

Just wait for the perfect time, a few more seconds.
Now!

Julie poured her second cup of coffee, settled on the couch and clicked on the television. She had just gotten home after working third shift at the hospital. The children had already left for school hours before she arrived home and John was at the restaurant going over the sales numbers from the previous month with Red. She sat back and turned on a daily news program. The Seattle Slayer case was being spotlighted on the show, as the national intrigue had increased with each abduction. She saw John and his new partner Ricky on a video showing the rescue of Brian Simmons. Though she didn't like the idea of John still working as a detective, she couldn't help but feel a bit of pride when she saw his handsome face on the national news. She was listening to an interview with Captain Johnson and an FBI agent when her cellphone rang. She saw it was the school calling.

"Hello?"

"Hi, Mrs. Corbin?"

"Yes."

"Neither Gianna or Ryann came to school today and we have no record of a parent calling. Our policy is to call the guardian by this time if we haven't heard from them."

"What? They aren't in school?" Where...? I have to go."

She hung up the phone as an instinctive feeling of panic came over her.

Captain Johnson entered his office, sat down, and clicked on his email. There was a new message with a lone hyperlink. He closed his eyes, said a quick prayer and clicked. A video came to life. It showed a long, dark tunnel-like structure. As the wind kicked up, he noticed two kids back to back on what seemed to be a platform. He zoomed in on the platform. He could hear the children crying now as the wind died down. He zoomed in even more and noticed the children had nooses around their necks attached to the ceiling.

"What the fuck..." he said aloud as one of the children turned towards the camera.

"Oh no. Oh no, no, no..."

CHAPTER SIX

24:00:00, 23:59:59, 23:59:58...

The captain couldn't believe what he was seeing: John's children, Gianna and Ryann, both secured on the platform with nooses around their necks. He zoomed in enough to see the trapdoor they stood upon. In less than twenty-four hours, John's children would be hung. He picked up the phone and hit Ricky's extension.

"Ricky, get in here," he said hoarsely, "I've got another video."

"I'll be right in."

Captain Johnson leaned back in his chair as Ricky entered the office and walked over to look at the screen.

"Children? What the fuck."

"Not just any children. Those are John's kids."

"*What?* Are you fucking kidding me?"

As Captain Johnson zoomed in on the children's faces again, Ricky brought his hands to his face, shook his head and bent over to regain his composure.

"Where's John?" Captain Johnson asked.

"At the restaurant taking care of some paperwork with Red."

"We need to tell him, but I don't want him to see this feed... that's enough to drive any man insane. I also want him off this case. I want you take lead."

"Captain, you know he won't accept that — it's his kids."

"He won't do us any good with an overload of emotion, and there is no way in hell for him to control that. We need to save them, and having someone make bad decisions based on emotion isn't going to help us do that."

"I agree, but how are we going to convince him of that?"

"I'm the captain. He has no choice but to follow my orders. He can hate me all he wants for now, but I need to do what's right for him, us, and those children."

"Do you want me to talk to him? I can—"

"No," The captain said curtly, interrupting him. "I'll head over there and handle this myself." The captain got up and headed out the door.

Ricky just stood there, watching the scene in disbelief.

23:45:03, 23:45:02, 23:45:01...

John sat in his office with Red, entering the sales and overhead costs into his computer when his cell tone went off.

"Hold on, Red, it's Julie. Hey babe, what's up? You should be sleeping."

"John, are the children with you?"

"No, why? What do you mean with me? They went to school."

"The school called and they aren't there. Where the hell could they be?"

As John got up to leave, Captain Johnson walked into the office. "John, sit down."

"My children never made it to school, I have to go..."

"John, I know where they are."

"What? What are you talking about? Julie, I'll call you right back." John hung up before she could reply.

"Red, please get John a drink. Something strong, preferably."

"Sure," Red said, and walked out of the office.

The Captain sat down. "John, I received a video link fifteen minutes ago. He has your children."

John looked at his captain with a blank stare until what was said sank in.

"What?"

"We'll find them. Me, Ricky, and the feds. You have to trust us."

"I'm going with you," John said, standing up.

Red walked in with a scotch on the rocks, "Here John, drink up."

"John, you're not working this case. I'm sorry."

"The fuck I'm not. You can't stop me."

"John, if you were me, what would you do? You would keep yourself from it. It's too close to your heart. You know as well as anyone that doesn't mix. I'm making this decision for you and your children. We'll find them, just trust us and accept our help."

"I want to see..."

"John, I don't think that's a good —"

"I WANT TO SEE THEM, GODDAMIT!"

The Captain sighed, dropped his head and said, "Okay, but on one condition. You let us handle it. Go be with your wife. She needs you right now. Promise me that, and I'll take you to see them."

John looked at the captain. "Okay, I promise."

23:22:03, 23:22,02, 23:22:01...

On the way back to the station, John called Julie and she answered on the first ring.

"John?"

"Yes. Julie listen, he has them. The killer has them. I'm going to the station now to see the video feed and then I'll come home."

"What?"

"He has Gianna and Ryann. I'm sorry," John heard those useless words spoken from him, and there was no answer from his wife. He heard his wife's sobs as he felt pain arise in his heart.

"Julie, are you there?" Again, nothing. "Listen, I'll make this right." The captain glanced over as he drove.

Finally, she answered. "You did this. You just had to jump back in. Why, John? We had everything we needed. *Why*?"

"I'll save them... I have to," John said to an empty line. Julie had hung up.

They arrived at the station and John rushed into the office and brought up the video feed. There, on a small platform, were his babies, each with a noose around the neck. He heard the muffled cries through the wind that had started to kick up. As the captain finally caught up to him and walked into the office, John dropped to his knees and brought his hands to his face.

"*Noooooo!*" he screamed as Captain Johnson put his hand on his shoulder.

23:04:03, 23:04:02, 23:04:01...

Ricky walked into the office and he and the captain attempted to comfort John any way they could.

"John, I don't have to tell you we'll do everything in our power to get them back. I'll put all of my manpower on this case," Captain Johnson said. "Let me take you home. You need to go be with Julie. Your wife needs you now more than ever. I'll take you."

"If I agree to go home now, will I be allowed back to work on the case?"

The captain glanced at Ricky who turned to John. "Let us do our jobs. We'll get them back, trust us. You know it's the correct way to handle this."

"Promise me or I'm not going."

"John..."

"Promise me goddamnit!"

"Okay! I'll let you come back, but not to work the case. You can return but let us do our jobs. It's what best for everyone involved," Captain Johnson said.

Ricky watched as the captain walked John out of the station. He then turned his attention to the video feed. It was a very dark, shadowy place; very high ceiling, maybe fifteen feet or more. He zoomed in on the platform and noticed the trapdoor. "Bastard is going to hang them, crazy son of a bitch."

Ricky took out his notebook and jotted down all the characteristics of the scene: large dark enclosure with a high ceiling, a wooden platform set up like gallows, a noose around each of the kid's necks. He turned the sound up and he heard the wind pick up and whip by the camera. Then he heard the cries, the cries of the innocent, just like in his dreams.

22:45:03, 22:45:02, 22:45:01...

John entered his house to a warm welcome from Simba. John shut the door, sat down on the floor, and held his loyal canine close to him. Simba licked away his tears as John tried to regain control. He stood and walked upstairs to find his wife. Julie was face down on the bed in her panties and a t-shirt. He walked into the bathroom to quickly wash his face with cold water. He saw the bathroom mirror shattered, vomit on the floor and toilet seat, and noticed the empty wine bottle on the floor. He walked over and flushed the toilet, grabbed a towel, and wiped up what he could. He then noticed the blood in the sink. He rushed from the bathroom to the bed.

"Julie, are you okay?"

No answer, so he walked around to her side of the bed. She had a blood-soaked towel on her right hand. John gently unwrapped the towel to expose a deep gash on the side of her hand.

"Julie?"

"Get away from me."

"Julie, what the hell did you do? You need stitches. I'll take you."

"I punched the mirror. Get the hell away from me and don't come back until you have our children."

"Julie, I—"

"*Leave now, you son of a bitch!*" she screamed as she jumped up and swung her good hand at his head. John ducked and wrapped his arms around her.

"I'm sorry. I'll make it right, I'll save them. Julie, I love you. I'm sorry."

She started sobbing and relented to his embrace. Finally, she put her head to his chest and let go. She cried in deep, horrible, heart-wrenching sobs, a dark and hollow cry that emanates from the soul and squeezes your heart in a vice of sorrow. Soon, John was crying with her and all he could do was hold and comfort her as best he could. After what seemed an eternity she stopped, looked up into his eyes and said, "John, you have to get them back."

He looked into her bloodshot eyes and answered, "I will..."

22:20:03, 22:20:02, 22:20:01...

Ryann stopped crying and turned to speak to his sister. "Gianna, what's happening? Is daddy coming to get us?"

"Yes, Ryann, we'll be fine. I'm sure Dad is working on finding us right now and may even be on his way."

"Where are we?"

"I don't know. Maybe a tunnel of some sort. What can you see from your side?"

"Just the wall in front of me, the rest is too dark to see. This thing around my neck hurts, it's too tight. Is he going to... hang us?"

"No, we're going to escape. Ryann, try to get loose from the restraints on your wrists."

"Okay."

Gianna glanced up, turned and noticed the small light from the camera. She turned back and worked on her own restraints. The wind kicked up, blowing her hair in her face as she felt the noose tighten, ever so gently.

22:05:03, 22:05:02, 22:05:01...

Ricky sat at his desk, searching the Internet for any structures that may fit the characteristics of the scene he had written in his notebook. The captain was outside talking to the press who, thankfully, hadn't gotten any information about the children. It would only be a matter of time because that's how these things worked. Ricky was a relatively inexperienced detective, but he already knew there were agents with connections who would leak info to the press for future favors. He glanced up as he saw Alexis walk into the station and up to his desk.

"Hi, how are you? How's your dad?" Ricky asked.

"We're as well as can be expected, thank you. I was wondering if you would like to grab lunch with me."

"Oh, I would love to, but something has come up," he answered.

"What? Anything I can help you with?"

Ricky glanced around, deeply sighed and said, "Follow me into the captain's office."

As she followed him across the station to the office, Ricky wondered to himself why he had no self-control whenever it came to this woman. He closed the door behind them and took her in his arms.

"I've missed you. Listen, what I'm about to show you cannot leave this room. Deal?"

"I've missed you as well, Ricky. You know I would never do anything to cause a problem for you."

"Okay," Ricky said as he sat at the computer and turned the monitor toward Alexis. He zoomed in on the platform.

"Oh my, they're just children! Is he going to hang them?"

"Unless we can stop him, I'm positive he'll do just that. But those aren't just any children, they're John's children." Alexis quickly brought a hand to her mouth and let out a squeal. "Alexis, there's something I have to tell you. John saved your father. He deciphered the riddle. I need to save his children; not just to repay him, but because I can't let him go through the horror of losing them. He's a great man, excellent detective, and wonderful father who loves his family more than anything in the world."

Alexis' eyes started to tear up as she studied the scene on the monitor. "Ricky, is there anything I can do?"

"Pray, if you believe in that sort of thing." Ricky looked up and saw the congregation on the street in front of the station start to break up. "If not, I guess we can always start. I mean, what could it hurt, right?"

Alexis hugged him, and Ricky held her head to his chest.

20:00:03, 20:00:02, 20:00:01…

John had taken Julie to the hospital to get the couple of stitches she needed to close the small gash on the side of her hand. As soon as Doctor Talbot noticed Julie in the ER, he immediately brought her into his room, cleaned, and stitched her wound. When they returned home, Julie immediately collapsed on the couch, exhausted from her emotional distress. John went to the bedroom and opened the bottom drawer of the dresser, the drawer Julie used to store their bible. John picked the book up and studied the cover. He opened the pristine pages and leafed through them, glancing over the text. John's mind wandered:

We all would like to believe the faith and spirit of our souls will guide us through life, unscathed and protected, but the somber truth is we are just matter, ushered along in a world of physical substance governed by the rules and guidelines of our universe and its uncertain, unpredictable laws. A plane crash here, a terminal disease there, for no rhyme or reason, eradicating people just because they pulled a joker from the deck or obtained a pair of snake eyes on one roll of the dice. Well fuck you fate, and fuck you, God…

John slammed the book shut and tossed it into the trash bin in the bathroom. He glanced into the part of the mirror still intact. His reflection, with the cracks of what remained running through his face, accurately portrayed how he felt. He was a broken man, and if he lost his children, he wasn't sure if he would ever put himself back together again. He headed downstairs, wrote Julie a note for when she woke, and headed for the station.

19:42:03, 19:42:02, 19:42:01…

John arrived and entered Captain Johnson's office where Ricky was studying the video feed. John sat next to him and saw his children with their heads down, nooses still secure, waiting for their execution.

"John, how is she?" Ricky asked, more to break the silence than in wanting an answer.

"She's a mess. Punched the mirror, had to get stitches. She passed out on the couch."

"I can't imagine. I'm so sorry."

"It's a hard feeling to explain. Once you have a child, you change. You're no longer free. The constant pressures and fears bind you in chains that only your heart can see or feel. When those horrific fears come true, it's surreal, like living in a nightmare. Ricky, have you ever felt your core shake? Have you ever been hit with so much emotional turmoil that everything becomes fuzzy and trancelike? Your lungs feel tight and you can't do anything. You're unable to move, unable to react, unable to even think. That's what I have felt since I found out he has my kids."

"We'll get them. I promise you with my life. Just trust us."

"Any idea where they are?"

"Not yet, but I'm working on a few theories. Go grab a drink and come back in a few hours. Watching them suffer will only make things worse."

"You're right. I need to inform Red anyway. A drink will help numb my mind."

"Of course. Come back in a few hours… maybe I'll have something by then."

John stood, placed his hand on Ricky's shoulder, and walked out.

19:20:03, 19:20:02, 19:20:01...

John sat at the bar of his own restaurant with every intention of drinking himself numb; a numbness that would save him from the horrors of the world he gave so much to over the years. Red was working the floor, but when he saw John he approached his friend and sat down next to him.

"I heard. Captain Johnson sent me the details. John, I'm sorry."

"Me too, Red, me too. I need a drink."

"Sure, scotch on the rocks?"

"Yes, please."

Red made his drink and returned to the seat next to John. "How's Julie?"

"She's a mess. Blames me, and rightfully so. If I had just stayed away, none of this would be happening."

"You don't know that. This maniac searched you out. This whole production; the emails, the videos, the twisted traps, they're all for you, John. He would have found you one way or another."

"Maybe, maybe not, but I need to find him and end this. I swear to hell, Red, I will kill him, just like the others. Just like Silas Alvah."

"John, you're past that. Don't go back, go forward. You're a better man than that now. You must fight those instincts. If not for him, then for you, Julie, and your kids."

John downed his drink and pushed his glass to Richard, the bartender who had just arrived for his shift.

"Scotch on the rocks please, Richard."

"Coming right up."

"John, don't drink too much, you need to be thinking straight in case they need your help," Red said.

"The captain gave me a leave. He thinks I'd hinder them, not help."

"Well, he may be right about that. Trust in them, they're good men and great detectives."

"It's weird, Red. When I think about my children, it's never how they are now. I see them in stages of their lives, growing up. I'll never forget how they looked as infants, as toddlers. I've a message on my voicemail that I saved from Gianna when she was about seven. It was on Halloween and she was calling to make sure we were still going on a haunted hayride. She sounds so pure, innocent, but yet so brave. She was always so courageous, never afraid of anything. She made me so proud. I listen to that message every now and then just to go back to that time. Sound does that to us. It can take us back to certain moments and make them seem genuine and real."

"They'll find your children. Just have faith."

"Faith? Don't be a prisoner of that beautiful lie, Red. People would rather believe a comforting fable than accept a painful truth, and this painful truth is I may have lost my children forever."

After another drink, Red took John home. He walked in and sat by his wife, who was still asleep on the couch. He was soon fast asleep himself, his mind exhausted and inebriated.

18:05:03, 18:05:02, 18:05:01...

Ricky researched the web for any landmarks in or around Seattle that fit the scene from the video: a tunnel-like structure maybe twenty-five feet wide and fifteen feet high. Because of the grainy, dark video, there wasn't much else to discern, other than those approximate measurements. The ceiling and the walls were hard to see, and the video cut off just above the ground. *The son of a bitch was careful not to give away any clues through the video,* Ricky thought as Captain Johnson walked up to his desk.

"Anything?" he asked.

"I've done an Internet search on all of the tunnels, underpasses, subways, mines, burrows, shafts, and passageways in or around the Seattle area. I need you to take a look and eliminate the ones that don't fit what our video shows. I don't know this area as well as you, so your help decreasing the possibilities will save valuable time. Here's a list I printed out. "

"Sure, I'll be back in a few," the captain said as he grabbed the list and headed for his office.

16:10:03, 16:10:02, 16:10:01...

John watched as his two newborn babies wriggled in their bassinets. They each donned a little cap, the girl's pink and the boy's blue. They were the most beautiful sights he had ever taken in. Suddenly there was movement from the corner of the room. Shadows danced and something shifted just outside of John's vision.

"Who's there?" He asked as he peered through the glass. He noticed what looked like a man's silhouette against the far wall, move forward, moving toward the bassinettes which contained his babies. As the light reflected on the figure, he noticed it wasn't walking, but floating on air. He also realized it was no man. The creature had a man's face, but any human resemblance ended there. It sported two horns that spiral up above its head, beady red eyes, and ragged black wings that fluttered behind it as it levitated across the room. Before turning its ugly head towards the babies, it looked straight at John and smiled, revealing a vile set of razor-sharp, jagged yellow teeth. John started screaming and pounding on the glass. It was to no avail as it was impenetrable. He heard the newborns harrowing screams as blood splattered on the floor, walls, and ceiling. The beast turned with a little foot hanging out of its mouth, and it continued to chew until the extremity was gone. Blood covered its evil mouth and a long, black forked tongue protruded from the mouth to lick it up. John screamed and continued to pound on the partition. The creature floated slowly over to the glass and looked John in the eyes. With only a couple of feet between them, the beast threw its head back and let out the most chilling, evil laugh John had ever heard. John dropped to his knees with his face in his hands...

He awoke in a cold sweat, confused and horrified. Slowly, the real world returned and instead of relieving him of his horrors, it just traded one for another. His real children were out there somewhere, their fate held in the hands of a psychotic lunatic. John rolled off the couch and for the first time realized Julie wasn't with him. He stood and walked upstairs to the bedroom, stopping at the doorway. She was on the bed, asleep with an empty wine bottle in her hand. John walked over and took the bottle from her. He then emptied the house of whatever alcohol it contained. When done, he headed out the door for the station, the residue of his horrific dream still on his mind.

15:58:03, 15:58:02, 15:58:01…

Captain Johnson returned to Ricky with the majority of the list slashed.

"Most of these sights are either still in operation or don't fit the physical properties of the scene in the video. The ones I've left are all possible sites, however, there is a something that may throw a wrench in your search."

"What's that?" Ricky asked.

"Have you ever heard of the Seattle Underground?"

"The Seattle Underground? No, what the hell is that?"

"Seattle's original buildings were all built using wood. In 1889, a cabinet maker accidentally overturned and ignited a glue pot. The attempt to extinguish the fire spread the burning grease over thirty-one blocks. Instead of rebuilding the city as before, all the new buildings were made of stone and brick. They also re-graded the streets one to two stories higher than the original street grade, creating a series of underground passageways and catacombs. In 1907, the city condemned the Underground for fear of the Bubonic Plague. It was left to deteriorate and rot, often being used as illegal flophouses for the homeless. A small portion has been restored and is now used for guided tours, but there's a whole network down there that's uninhabited and empty. There's a possibility that's where

John's children are being held. There're other possibilities out there, but that's where we'll start."

"This city gets creepier and creepier with every day that goes by," Ricky said.

"As well as its inhabitants. I'm going to get access down there and send a search party to scour the whole place. I know it isn't safe, so we'll have to take precautions that'll slow down the hunt. I'll get the feds on board also." Captain Johnson left the papers on Ricky's desk and headed for the room used as the FBI's headquarters.

Ricky typed "Seattle Underground" into his computer's search engine. An assortment of eerie pictures and stories came up. He let out a deep breath and clicked on the first one.

15:22:03, 15:22:02, 15:22:01...

Alexis walked her father down the steps of Harbor View Hospital and into the passenger seat of her waiting car.

"Before you drop me off at my place, take me to a liquor store. I need to stock up on some spirits if I'm going to be immobile for a while."

Alexis hopped into the driver's seat, smirked, and said, "Dad, no way. You're staying with me until I feel you're strong enough to be alone again. Also, the booze binges are over. I'll help you break your dependency and get clean. Together, you and I will defeat it, *if* you promise me your full effort."

Brian Simmons looked at his daughter with love in his eyes. He would rather die than let her down again. "Alexis, I promise you my full effort."

Alexis smiled and pulled into the flow of the traffic and headed home.

15:09:03, 15:09:02, 15:09:01...

The dark figure watched the two children as they stood on the platform, back to back, waiting to have their necks snapped. His mind turned as he contemplated the scene. *Must be such a terrifying, morbid existence for children, not yet really understanding the world and its intricacies and complications. Left there to hang, with only each other for comfort, so sad.*

He threw his head back and laughed. Not a chuckle, but a full-bodied laugh that started in his eyes and ended in his stomach. The fit of enjoyment made him realize his belly was empty. He headed to the kitchen to make himself a peanut butter sandwich. The dark figure didn't eat meat, as he thought it barbaric and inhumane. He finished making his meal and sat down in front of the computer to enjoy the entertainment, as he filled his empty stomach.

14:40:03, 14:40:02, 14:40:01...

John sat in Captain Johnson's chair watching his children who looked frightened, exhausted, and hopeless. Ricky walked in the office and put his hand on John's shoulder before sitting down next to him.

"We have some leads we're working on."

"What are they?"

"First, the Seattle Underground. Have you ever been down there?"

"No, how did you come up with that?"

"The captain said it makes sense. It's pretty abandoned and dark, and it fits the video feed scenario."

"I don't know, it looks more like an enclosed tunnel of some sort."

"There's a network of catacombs and passages down there," Ricky said as John's stare left the screen and was now focused on Ricky. "I did some research." Ricky shrugged his shoulders. "The captain's organizing a unit of feds, swat, and detectives to search it as we speak. We should be ready to go live anytime."

"What other theories?"

"Stampede Pass, Fort Lawton Tunnel... there are also quite a few sewer tunnels. We're still researching all of the railroad tunnels and finding out which ones aren't in operation anymore."

"I want to be in on every search. I want to be there to save them when we find them."

"John... I'm not sure—"

John kicked back in the chair and turned to look at his partner. "Ricky, don't. This is my life. This is everything Julie and I live for. Without them, we're finished — as a couple, and as individuals. If you're my partner and friend, I'd like you to take me there. If you refuse, I'll go myself."

Ricky glanced back at the screen. "I understand, I'll take you wherever this leads us."

"Thank you."

"I can't imagine what you two are going through, John. I'm sorry."

"This is what you sign on for, as a cop and as a parent. Having children is accepting a vulnerability that just isn't there otherwise. It's sacrificing your right to be happy, if it turns out that way. The fear, the constant worry of something hurting them, never goes away, remember that. If you choose to father a child someday, it could be you sitting in this chair watching him or her on a video. You could be the one comforting your wife as she drinks herself into oblivion because she can't face the reality of what's happening."

Ricky just watched the video and remained silent until the captain called on his radio.

"Ricky, we got clearance, we're going in. Meet me there in twenty minutes."

"Got it," Ricky answered as he looked at John. "You ready for this?"

John stood up and turned off the monitor.

"Let's go."

14:10:03, 14:10:02, 14:10:01...

Ricky glanced over at John as he drove them on the short trip from police headquarters to Pioneer Square. He noticed how fatigued he looked. John had always looked young and spry for his age, but now Ricky could easily make out the dark circles under his eyes, the stress lines that had become more defined overnight, and his disheveled hair which hadn't been brushed in over a day. A feeling of despair struck his heart knowing his friend was in such pain. He turned his attention back to the road as he pulled onto Yesler Way in Pioneer Square. Moments later he turned onto 1st Ave and pulled up to the edge of the curb in front of the building used as the entrance to the underground tour. A mix of detectives, uniformed officers, and feds were already present and heading in two at a time to join the search. The partners got out and walked up to the captain who was standing by the door leading underground.

"John, how's Julie?"

"Terrible, how many do we have searching?"

"All I had available and some feds. That's about forty, total. We estimate it'll take an hour for a thorough search, maybe a bit longer depending on how they can move down there. Some parts haven't seen a human in years."

The sun had set, enveloping the Seattle landscape in a dark, haunting hue, somewhere between dusk and the pitch-black darkness of midnight. John stepped outside and took a deep breath as he glanced up at the brilliant full moon and said a prayer in his mind to no one in particular. If this search failed, would he be able to rekindle his hope, or would he be emotionally crushed? He watched the final members of the force file into the underground. These were his brethren, his brothers, and they all knew what the stakes were in this case. They worked with an intensity and vigor that John respected and appreciated. The goal was always to save the innocent, but the rare times their profession touched their personal lives, the rest of the force would give that little extra to achieve their desired result.

"Doing okay out here?" Ricky asked as he walked outside.

"Just getting some air, anything yet?"

"No, most have just entered. I'll be going in with Officer Connor shortly. The captain is organizing the map so we cover all of the areas as efficiently as possible. If your children are under there, we'll find them, partner."

"If they're found, I want to be the first to know. I want to be there to escort them out."

"Understood."

Ricky patted John on the back and headed inside to begin his search. John's eyes wandered back to the glowing round orb overlooking Western Seattle.

13:02:03, 13:02:02, 13:02:01…

John stood inside a makeshift office just outside the entrance to the underground and waited for a report, any report, of a rescue. Countless teams had checked in by radio with negative results. The captain stood over a map of the underground marking each portion that was vacant with a red X. With ever report returned to them, the chances of this being the site decreased. Captain Johnson glanced at John with a slight frown on his face.

"How many sections are left?" John asked.

"Four. It's not looking good, John."

As John heard the last four search parties report in, he got up and walked outside. He turned to find the beautiful, glowing moon high in the night sky, but a cloud cover had moved in and left a lonely, overcast, gloomy cover. A small tear fell from his eye as he walked to Ricky's car, got in and laid his head back on the rest. Moments later, Ricky entered and drove them back to the station. No words were spoken. None were needed.

12:24:03, 12:24:02, 12:24:01...

Back at the station, the mood was somber. Captain Johnson sent out search parties to other possible sights, but with little confidence of success. John had spent ten minutes alone in the bathroom vomiting. When he came out he looked as pale and withdrawn as a ghost, an unhealthy one at that. After John informed Ricky of his wife's wine binge, Ricky sent an officer by John's house to check on her. He reported back confirming that her car was still in the driveway, and the house was dark other than the foyer light on the first floor, so Ricky assumed she was still in bed, passed out. Captain Johnson stepped in with the feds to work on a map of Seattle containing possible areas that matched whatever clues the video displayed.

"Hang in there, a few more minutes and we'll have something to work on, hopefully containing a missing link," Ricky said as John sat next to him with his head in his hands. John nodded his head and Ricky noticed a tremble in his movements that he'd never seen from John before. At that moment, he understood the depth of love that people feel for their children. He felt an ache start in the base of his skull and he leaned back to release some strain and pressure.

"How's Alexis?" John asked, and Ricky's head shot straight up, startled to hear him speak.

"She's great, John. We are great."

"Ricky, I can't stress this enough; the people, the monsters we deal with doing this job are evil and we put our loved ones at risk every time we investigate a case. Don't follow in my footsteps. If you want to have a family, move on to a different career. I tried but then I got weak and fucked it up."

"I'm a detective, just like you are. The passion to do this job is anchored to our souls. We can't just change. Partner, none of this is your fault—"

John stuck his hand up to stop Ricky mid-sentence. "It is. You know it and I know it. My choices led to this. Different choices, different outcome, meaning my children should be at home in bed right now instead of in some cold dark place, waiting to be hung."

"Stay with me, partner, don't lose hope. We'll find them. I'll find them if I have to search every possible area myself." For a moment their gazes met and there was an understanding reached that they would always have each other's back as long as they needed each other. John gave a slight nod to confirm he understood, and Ricky went back to work.

12:00:03, 12:00:02, 12:00:01...

Captain Johnson sat in front of the computer, waiting for the expected email containing a clue to the children's whereabouts to appear. Ricky sat next to him in anticipation while John sat on the floor, his back to the wall and his head in his hands. Suddenly, right on cue at twelve hours remaining, the email arrived:

আর t I s কى N ى اى A س O g M L O د R t A O n U টি A O انا E i R ايل f L I n O N a تى

Two rows of assorted text appeared all in the color of blood red. The trio sat and absorbed the text before any dared to speak. They all had learned over the years that reacting too quickly usually leads to mistakes and wasted time. Patience and an analytical, organized thought process led to success. Captain Johnson was the first to speak.

"My God, what the fuck is that?"

"I don't think God has been around these parts for quite some time," John replied.

"It must be scrambled letters, like the word scramble games they have in the back of the newspapers. Some are obviously in foreign languages."

"Must be, but there are nine lowercase letters," Ricky observed.

John had gotten up and was now studying the text over Ricky's shoulder. "There is software that can unscramble letters to make any words that are possible from the group of letters. This seems to be a combination of words with quite a few possibilities. Also, they're all red."

"I'm forwarding it to the feds. We'll need an interpreter. Looks like a few different languages," Captain Johnson said, then headed for their office across the hall.

"I'm going to download the software we need to unscramble this mess," Ricky said. John got up and paced the room, burning off some nervous energy. Suddenly, John was overwhelmed with the reality of what was happening. His thoughts turned in his mind like clothes in a dryer; his children, his wife, who was responsible for all of this... but why? He felt a wave of bile erupt from his esophagus and enter his mouth. He rushed to the bathroom and spit the rancid juices into the sink as the beginning symptoms of a migraine started to surface. A dull ache had started in his neck and he became lightheaded and dizzy. His vision blurred, and the light hurt his eyes. A sharp pain took over the base of his head and started to work its way up his skull. John flipped off the light and sat on the bathroom tile with his back against the wall.

Moments later he was unconscious.

11:36:03, 11:36:02, 11:36:01...

Julie awoke to a dull ache in her head and a mouth as dry as the Sahara Desert. She opened her eyes and for a moment, she was free of the tragedy in her life. Suddenly, reality returned like a brick to the back of her head and a knife into her heart. Her children were gone. She let out a small shriek and collapsed onto the bed again. She remained prone for another ten minutes before acquiring the courage to rise. She went to the bathroom to wash up. She then picked up her cell and called John. She needed to know where her children were. She needed to know if she could help in any way. There was no answer, so Julie threw the phone on the bed in disgust. She grabbed a jacket and made her way downstairs and out the front door toward her car, noticing the patrol car parked in front of her house. The driver's side door opened, and an officer approached her.

"Ma'am, I have instructions to keep you here, safe."

"I'm going to the station. You can stand in my way and get run over, or you can escort me there."

The officer nodded then entered his vehicle and pushed the passenger's side door open for her to join him.

"Thank you," she said as she got in and they pulled onto the road.

11:00:03, 11:00:02, 11:00:01...

Gianna licked her lips to moisten them with the small amount of saliva she had left in her mouth. Dehydration had started to set in and she started to feel light headed and nauseous. She imagined a tall glass of ice water and how good it would taste and feel going down her parched throat. She turned to look at her brother's face illuminated by the glow of the camera recording them. Ryann was deep asleep, which Gianna was thankful for. She wanted her little brother's suffering to be as limited as possible. She prayed her father was on his way to save them. As she looked toward the camera, a small tear escaped her eye. She had been holding in her sobs to appear strong for her brother, but now that he was asleep, she had to weep a bit. She was scared of dying. She was frightened of being hung like she saw in the movies. *What if dad doesn't make it in time? What if we die of thirst? What if the platform opens and our necks snap? What if...?*

10:52:03, 10:52:02, 10:52:01...

The captain looked up to see Julie Corbin walk into the station. He hurried over to her and gave her a hug.

"Julie, I'm so sorry. We're doing everything we can and are confident we will find them."

"Thank you, Michael. Where is John?"

"He is in my office with Detective Barnes. Julie, wait..." Captain Johnson said as Julie made a hasty charge for the office. He followed her as she entered the room.

"Mrs. Corbin, John left about an hour ago," Ricky said.

"Detective Barnes, his truck is still here," she replied.

Ricky gave her a puzzled look as Captain Johnson walked in to join them.

"Is he in the kitchen or waiting room?"

"I'll check. Follow me, Julie," the captain said as he walked out.

They searched the station, but to no avail. Julie then saw the door to the men's bathroom. She knocked before pushing it open.

10:38:03, 10:38:02, 10:38:01...

Julie saw her husband unconscious on the floor and panic overtook her.

"John!" she yelled as she dropped down beside him and took his face in her hands. He was cold to the touch and his skin had a clammy feel to it. Rosalie rushed in and quickly soaked a towel in cold water and applied it to John's neck, head, and face. After a few swabs, John slowly opened his eyes.

"What? Where...?"

"Shhh, just lay back," Julie said. She held him and continued running the cold towel over him. Slowly, his color returned, and he tried to stand.

"Our children!"

"Hold on, John. Go slow. You're dehydrated and close to exhaustion." Rosalie returned with a glass of cold water. She proceeded to take John's blood pressure and temperature.

"Are you a nurse?" Julie asked.

"Well, no, but I could be. I studied nursing for three years after my mother died, I didn't have the energy nor drive to continue, so I got a job here through my cousin, Officer Conti. He's retired now, but I stayed. I always bring my medical supplies with me and keep them in my car or here at the station. You never know when something is needed. John, you've a slight fever and your blood pressure is elevated. You need to rest, eat, and drink something."

"I can't eat," he said simply.

"Then drink something with some calories and nutrients. You're going to get seriously ill if you continue down this road. Promise me you will."

"Okay, I promise."

"Good boy, I'll get you some juice, just stay here for a bit until you regain some strength." She stood and walked out of the bathroom.

"John, are you okay? Feeling any better?" Julie asked.

'I'm fine, help me up.'

"Not until you drink some juice like she said." Julie got up and met Rosalie at the door and took the tall glass of juice offered. "Thank you."

"You're welcome. I need to go back to work. Take care of him."

"Will do," Julie said as she took the glass to her husband.

9:53:03, 9:53:02, 9:53:01...

John rallied and regained his strength. As he and Julie sat together in the waiting room, Ricky and Captain Johnson were working hard to decipher the text. There were hundreds of possible words that could be interpreted from the given letters. As they ran them through the database, nothing seemed to click as a possible hint to the site where the children were being held. The feds interpreter had just arrived and was deciphering the foreign letters.

"This is nearly impossible," Ricky said to the captain with a shake of his head. "There may be extra letters here just to throw us off... how would we know?" As he studied the text, something that now seemed fairly obvious occurred to him. "The lowercase letters, they may be reversed. I bet they're uppercase and the first letters of words in the hidden text."

"You may be right. Let's run all of the possible words starting with those letters against the database throughout Washington."

"I'm on it." Ricky rushed back to his computer to run the data. Captain Johnson stood in front of his desk, gazing at the row of letters.

"We'll figure this out, you son of a bitch. Then we're coming for you."

9:01:03, 9:01:02, 9:01:01...

Gianna was able to loosen one loop in the knot around her wrists. She pulled the rope through and continued to work on the rest. She hadn't heard her younger brother move or talk in quite a while, so she assumed he'd fallen back asleep. She was exhausted, hungry, thirsty, and weakening by the minute. She yanked another loop through and for the first time felt like she may be able to break free of the binds. She fought and struggled with the rope until she felt her hands slip free and the rope drop. She immediately went to work on the noose around her neck. She loosened it enough to slip it over her head. She took a step toward her brother when her feet suddenly gave way and she landed on the ground. She screamed as she saw Ryann's body jerk as the noose around his neck tighten and his feet dangling three feet off the ground, kicking wildly. She quickly got up and tried to lift his body to alleviate the pressure from his neck. She heard his neck snap as she dropped to the ground in tears. The last thing she heard was her little brother calling her name for help: "Gianna! Gianna! Gianna!"

She opened her eyes and turned to Ryann who had been screaming her name.

"Gianna, are you awake?"

"Yes, Ryann, I am now. What's wrong?"

"I was scared and alone. Don't fall asleep again."

"I'll try to stay awake," she replied.

"I'm thirsty."

"Me too, but we have to fight. Daddy is coming, I know it."

A steady breeze kicked up from the dark far corner of the tunnel, sending a chill through her body. The whole scene was dark now except for the glowing light of the camera pointed at them.

8:02:03, 8:02:02, 8:02:01...

The dark figure watched the children on the screen as he sat back and opened a drawer on the desk. He reached in and picked up an old photograph, which was frayed and worn. It was a young couple, sitting on the steps of a church. The man was glancing down at the beautiful woman with a look of intensity. Was it love that he saw in the man's eyes, or simple lust? The woman had a radiant smile on her lips as the sun shone down, illuminating the landscape into a scene that would look at home on a postcard or the cover of a book. He stared at her, memorizing every detail and every curve on the woman's face. The dark figure placed the picture next to the computer screen and smiled as he watched his two innocent captives struggle for their lives. *Suffering, failure, loneliness, sorrow, and death will be part of your journey, but the kingdom of God will never conquer all these horrors. The nefarious will resist grace forever until finally the divine fall to the shadow of evil.*

7:32:03, 7:32:02, 7:32:01...

The captain sat at his desk as Ricky walked in with a slew of pages in his hand.

"These are all of the possible words starting with the nine lower-case letters. I'm cross-referencing those words with all tunnels, passages, underpasses, burrows, mines or pits in Washington. Did the interpreters decipher the foreign letters?"

"Just finished, most are from the Middle East and Africa. Bengali, Dari, Urdu..."

"What the fuck is Urdu?" Ricky asked.

"It's a form of Hindustani, spoken in Pakistan."

"Okay, so what is the final sequence?"

"I will have it right about... now," Captain Johnson said as he pushed the enter button revealing the deciphered letters.

t l A s N E A Q O g M L O S R t R A O n U T A O l E i R L f L l n O N a T

"Well, that's much better. Send that to me and I'll go run a new cross-reference," Ricky said.

"On its way," the captain replied. "Ricky?"

Ricky stopped at the doorway and looked back at his boss.

"The answer is here, let's find it."

"I'm on it, sir," he answered and left to go to his computer.

6:48:03, 6:48:02, 6:48:01...

John and Julie sat and waited, their faith dwindling by the minute. Ricky had come to update them on the investigation moments ago. "We're zeroing in on some sites, while excluding many others," he had said. "Don't lose hope, I'm confident we'll solve it."

"Easy to keep hope when it's not your children," Julie said.

"I know, but he's right," John said softly. "We aren't defeated yet. I trust my people and what they do."

Julie put her hands together and placed them under her chin. She closed her eyes and bowed her head forward. John had only seen Julie pray a few times through their life together; once was when her father was rushed to the emergency room with acute abdominal pains. It turned out the distress was caused by an infected appendix that was removed and he was back home two days later. The other time was when their friend and John's partner, Todd McGrath, was shot during a shoot-out at the Northgate Mall. Julie was brought up Catholic, but her faith wasn't strong enough to bring her to church on Sundays. John always wondered about that contradiction and how many Catholics shared this part-time faith. Being a detective, John knew first-hand the thin, frail line between life and death was ruled by percentages, luck, and cause and effect. God, angels, or divine spirits couldn't save his children. They could only be saved by the blood, sweat, hard work, and intelligence of the people looking for them. He leaned back, shut his eyes and waited.

5:44:03, 5:44:02, 5:44:01...

Ricky had produced a list of Forty-two sites throughout Washington. He printed it and just as he was about to leave for the captain's office when he noticed Alexis walk into the station. He went to her and they embraced before heading to Ricky's desk.

"I'll only take a moment of your time," she said. "I came to check on you, John, and Julie and see how the investigation was going. Can I help in any way?"

"Thank you. If you would like to visit with John and Julie, they're in the back room. I'm sure they'll be happy to see you."

"I would love to see them. I'll stop in to say goodbye before I leave," Alexis said before hugging Ricky again and left. Ricky entered the office and handed Captain Johnson the list.

"This it?"

"Yes, we need to narrow it down, eliminate some sites. I'm sure many of these mines and tunnels are still in use or older ones have been destroyed recently, but this is where we will start."

"Sounds good. How's John?"

"He looks like hell. I'm worried what this will do to him in the long run. He has never looked so old."

"We're all eight-year-old souls walking around in decaying bodies. Nothing deteriorates our mental and physical well-being and puts us in the grave quicker than stress. John's a tough son-of-a-bitch, but everyone has their limits. He'll bounce back, but only if we find them."

"Well then, let's do just that."

3:32:03, 3:32:02, 3:32:01...

John left Alexis and Julie and headed for the captain's office. John noticed the two women had formed a small bond in the short time they had known each other. He walked in and sat next to Captain Johnson.

"How much time?

"Three and a half hours. We've made immense progress. Actually, here comes Ricky with the final printout."

"Guys, I've narrowed it down to two possible sites that fit the letters: The Great Northern Tunnel or The Iron Goat Trail. The Northern Tunnel has been temporarily closed for construction, but that has ceased for the last two months. The Iron Goat Trail has been closed and condemned for years. No other sites that fit the landscape of the video have letters that fit the text puzzle."

John sat up. "I know of it. Those are two tunnels that the Great Northern Railroad ran through."

"Exactly, that's the one."

John then looked at the text, all in red.

Son of a bitch.

"There is a red caboose that marks the start of that trail, it's a famous landmark. I've never been there, but I've seen pictures of it. It has to be The Iron Goat Trail Tunnels."

"I'm sending a team to The Great Northern Tunnel, I'll put a second team together for the Iron Goat Trail Tunnels," the captain said.

John noticed the glance in his direction when he mentioned putting a team together.

"Ricky, you take John with you. On the way, study maps to educate yourself on the trail. It will be very dark, so getting a head start on the landscape will only help."

"Will do, captain. John, let's go."

John looked at the captain as he rose to leave the office. "Thank you, sir." The captain nodded his head and walked out. The partners walked out of the office and the girls were waiting for them by Ricky's desk.

"John? Did you find out where they are?" Julie asked.

"We have a pretty good idea. We're leaving now. I'll call if we find them."

"No John," Julie said, looking steadily in his eyes. "Not if, when."

For the first time in almost a full day, a small hint of a smile flashed across his lips. "You're right... *when* we find them."

2:50:03, 2:50:02, 2:50:01...

As Ricky drove east on Route 90, John studied a map of the trails on his tablet.

"The trail contained two main tunnels: The Old Cascade Tunnel and the new, longer Second Cascade Tunnel. There are also a couple of smaller, shorter tunnels on the western side."

Ricky glanced over as he turned north onto I-405.

"Listen to this; 'This trail is the site of one of the worst railroad disasters in U.S. history. In 1910, an enormous avalanche on Windy Mountain swept two trains off the tracks into Tye Creek. The wreckage was horrific. Debris was strewn all over the mountain and into the creek. Ninety-six people lost their lives that night, only twenty-six survived. It took twelve days to dig the snow away from the tracks and the bodies were taken away by sled. The new Cascade Tunnel was completed in 1929, but the decaying tunnel remained, barely intact. There has been reported paranormal activity on the Iron Goat Trail. People have claimed to be touched by invisible hands, had their hair stand on end for no reason and even spotted apparitions. Some claim to have heard voices echoing through the tunnels, thought to be the screams and sobs of the people who gave their lives for the railroad.'"

Ricky glanced over at John. "Fucking wonderful. Now we have to deal with ghosts on top of a psychotic lunatic."

Moments later, Captain Johnson called over the radio. "Men, The Northern Tunnel is a negative. You will have forty men at your disposal. The feds have the lead on this. It's all you, boys."

Ricky thumbed the mic's call button. "We got it, over," Ricky said as he turned east onto WA-522 E. John glanced out the window into the night sky, noticing the bright twinkle in the stars. *Please, if you are out there, I need you to lead me to them. I need you, just this once.*

2:00:03, 2:00:02, 2:00:01...

Ricky turned left onto Old Cascade Highway and half a mile later, they were out of the vehicle and joining the squad at the meeting point. Agent Daniels immediately took control.

"I want four groups of ten men. Two groups take The First Cascade Tunnel, one starting on the east and the other from the west. The other two groups take The New Cascade Tunnel doing the same. It'll take a bit of time to hike to those points; we have spotlights that will help with the terrain. We have two hours, so let's get to it, men."

Ricky and John were in the group responsible for the west end of the old tunnel. They followed the Tye River north, through the mountains surrounded by a sea of evergreen and maple trees. At the end of the four-mile hike, they came to the clearing of The Wellington Trailhead. They set up a spotlight, which illuminated the west opening of the tunnel. John looked down and watched as a Pika nervously glanced at the group of men and scurried into a boxwood shrub. John glimpsed at Ricky and followed the team into the tunnel.

1:45:03, 1:45:02, 1:45:01...

At three miles long, the tunnel seemed narrow, dark, and endless. At places the deterioration was so bad it was almost impassable. At these disintegrating points, the men would work at removing debris to open an alley wide enough for the men to pass through. About a mile in, Ricky turned to John. "This isn't it, John."

"What makes you think so?" John asked as he glanced back at the dark outline of Ricky's face.

"Just a gut feeling. Someone taught me to follow that," Ricky said as he smirked at his mentor. "Stop a moment." The two men lagged behind the group. As the last of the team left their sight around a slight bend up ahead, Ricky said, "Quiet, listen. What do you hear?"

John closed his eyes and concentrated on listening. A few moments later he opened his eyes. "Nothing."

"Correct, what do you feel?"

"Tired, angry, hopeless."

"I mean physically."

"Nothing."

"Right, this isn't the tunnel," Ricky said.

John looked at Ricky as he shone his flashlight in his partners face.

"In the video, I could hear a faint wind. I remember your daughter's hair fluttering in the breeze every time I watched."

John turned towards the western end of the tunnel. "Let's go back. There are two smaller tunnels to the west."

Ricky nodded and glanced ahead to where their team had disappeared.

John followed his gaze and said, "No, let them go. We don't have time to discuss this with the feds. Every second matters."

Ricky nodded, turned back towards the west, and they re-tracked their steps and headed for the opening.

1:30:03, 1:30:02, 1:30:01…

As the pair exited the tunnel, they quickened their pace knowing they had a three-mile hike along the path. They knew time was running short, but they also knew a turned ankle or twisted knee would limit their speed, so they took every precaution to light up the ground with their flashlights as they walked. The night was black, even with the glow from the stars. They were surrounded by a darkness filled with strange noises and shadowy silhouettes of what they hoped were just trees and shrubbery.

John glanced down at the time on his watch. "Just under an hour and a half, we need to get moving."

They both hastened their gait as they worked their way on the down-slope of the mountainside. Suddenly, a high-pitched muffled snarl came from the north, maybe fifty yards away.

"What the fuck is that?" Ricky gasped.

"Sounds like a male cougar," John answered.

"How do you know it's male?"

"Well, it sounded big. Also, the females usually chirp like a bird to communicate with their young."

"Fucking cougars? I should have stayed in New York where all I had to deal with was felons on the run, street thugs, and terrorists." Ricky's face was sour.

"I'll stick with the cougars, thank you," John said.

Ricky flashed the light into the sea of trees to chase the cat away before continuing west toward the next tunnel.

1:00:03, 1:00:02, 1:00:01…

The path turned around a bend, and to their right was a huge concrete wall leading the path to the west. As they quickly sauntered around the turn, a crisp breeze hit them in the face. Ricky turned to John and nodded. John aimed his flashlight up ahead and there about fifty yards away was the opening to another tunnel. John broke into a full gallop as Ricky followed closely behind. They reached the opening and slowed down to a jog. John shined his light on a sign that warned hikers of the dangers of continuing past this point.

"How long is it?" Ricky asked as he slowed to a stop.

"Quarter mile; let's go," John answered.

John led the way, casting light on enough of the ground to advance safely as a gentle waft of air hit their faces. The deeper into the tunnel they ventured, the more it had decayed, with slabs of concrete missing from the walls and ceiling. After a ten-minute dash, John exited the west end, having found nothing. John was bent over at the waist in frustration as Ricky came through shortly after. He walked up to his friend and put his hand on his shoulder. "Come on, partner. We have one more chance."

30:03, 30:02, 30:01...

John knew they had another two-mile hike to reach the next and final tunnel. He quickly calculated how long it would take the average man to run a mile in ten minutes but with the precarious level of visibility, it would take a bit longer than that. With those calculations, he determined they would reach the beginning of the tunnel in twenty-five minutes, providing they were without any delays. That would leave five minutes to search the tunnel. He quickened up his pace to somewhere between a jog and an all-out sprint, hoping each step was true. Ricky followed suit, fast on John's heels. John heard a faint, throaty-cluck from above and glanced up to catch a night hawk in flight as it passed through the moons glow. John stumbled on a small depression, twisted his ankle a bit, but kept on running. He felt Ricky right behind him and heard his heavy breathing and his vigorous footsteps pounding the earth with his own. They ran up a small hill and down the slope of the other side and headed for a turn in the path to the north. John slowed to a walk and checked the time on his watch: 13:24. As he picked the pace back up into a frenzied sprint, he imagined his children in his mind; happy, innocent, and full of life and possibilities. At that moment, John ran harder and faster than he ever had before in his life.

8:03, 8:02, 8:01…

John raced around the bend, heading south-west and the path widened. He stopped and shone his light forward. Up ahead and maybe one-hundred yards away, was the opening. Half was closed off by debris, earth, rock, and shrubbery. Ricky caught up and slowed to a stop next to him. The wind picked up and whipped down the path towards the tunnel. They both broke into another gallop, knowing time was running out. They reached the mouth of the tunnel with just over seven minutes remaining. John moved some debris to give them a wider opening to walk through. They each squeezed through and John checked the time.

"Listen…" Ricky said, holding his finger to his lips. The small opening worked as a vacuum and they heard the whistle of the wind working through the circular tunnel. "This is it, John. Let's move."

1:03, 1:02, 1:01…

Gianna was losing hope. She and Ryann must have been here for at least a full day. Her stomach rumbled, her mouth was as dry as a desert, and she was growing weak. Ryann had fallen asleep again and she knew he was in rough shape. For the first time, doubt crept into her mind and a few tears fell as she slowly began to accept that her life may be over soon. Suddenly, she heard a sound echoing from around the bend in the tunnel. Her head shot up and her eyes quickly adjusted to the darkness behind the camera.

"Ryann! Wake up, someone is coming! Ryann!"

"Huh, what? Where…?

The silhouette of a man's running body appeared out of the shadows. She knew who it was before his face appeared out of the gloom and into focus: It was her father.

"Dad! Dad!" she screamed in exaltation, knowing that this nightmare would finally be over.

:30, :29, :28...

John sped around the bend and as he looked ahead saw the platform from the video maybe fifty yards away. He slowed a bit to check the time. Twenty-two seconds. He picked up his pace and called back to Ricky.

"They're here, hurry!" He heard the footsteps quicken and felt Ricky right behind him. "You grab Ryann and I'll grab Gianna!"

"Got it!" Ricky answered. They flew by the camera and both jumped onto the platform. John grabbed Gianna just under the waist and held her up. Suddenly half the platform fell away and John held on tight to his daughter. He moved his head around his daughter's body to get a view of his son. Ricky had him in his arms, safely suspended above the ground.

Ryann's eyes met his as he said, "Hi, Dad," and a wide smile appeared on his son's face.

CHAPTER SEVEN

John reached into his pocket with his free hand as he held his daughter up with the other. He grabbed his pocket knife, opened it up with one finger and started sawing the rope above his daughter's head. After a few moments, the rope gave way and he carried her off the platform. He set her down and climbed back up to free Ryann.

"Dad, thanks for coming and saving us," Ryann said as the second rope was sliced through and Ryann was free.

When John had both of his children safely on the ground his emotions let go and he cried as he held them both. He felt the wetness of Gianna's tears come through his shirt and he kissed her forehead. The depth and strength of his feelings reverberated through his soul. All he could think or feel was the love for his children and the relief of them being safe. Ricky walked away toward the mouth of the tunnel. He knew this precious moment was something John needed to share alone with his children.

"Daddy, I love you," Gianna said.

"I love you both so much. I'm so sorry this happened to you."

John stood and escorted the children out of the tunnel. When they reached the opening, medics ran up and quickly placed them both on stretchers then headed for the helicopter which would transport them to the hospital. John followed close behind as the light of the moon cascaded over the landscape in a radiant, joyous overlay. He pulled out his cell phone and called Julie.

"John?"

"We have them. They're safe." John heard the phone drop followed by Julie's sobs of happiness. After a moment, she regained her composure and continued.

"Where are they now?"

"They're taking them to the children's hospital. They need hydration and nutrients, but both are doing well."

"I'm on my way. John, I love you."

"I love you too."

John followed the medics to the trailhead parking lot where the helicopter awaited. They loaded the stretchers into the back of the copter and prepared to depart. Before John got in he saw Ricky talking to a few feds, including agent Daniels. He approached the group and interrupted their conversation by holding his hand out to his partner.

"Ricky, thank you. If not for you, my children would not be alive right now."

Ricky took his hand and hugged John. "My pleasure, I'm glad we found them."

John walked away from the group without saying another word and hopped into the helicopter.

John sat in room number 101, overlooking his sleeping children when Julie ran in.

"They're going to be fine," John said as he took his wife in his arms. Julie let go of her emotions and a stream of tears flowed as she held onto her husband.

"Doctor Steinberg said with some fluids and rest they'll be as good as new in a couple of days."

"Have they eaten?"

"No, he gave them nutrients intravenously and said they'll be able to eat in the morning." John paused and looked into her eyes. "Julie, there's something I need to tell you. I'm going to inform the captain that I'm done. I need to be home to protect you and the children right now. That's what's important."

"Thank you," Julie said as she held him tight and they both watched their children sleeping peacefully.

"You guys pissed off Daniels something fierce," Captain Johnson said. A soft chuckle escaped Ricky's mouth.

"Yeah, well if we had gotten into a pissing match, John's kids wouldn't be alive right now. Time was running out and I knew we were in the wrong tunnel. We didn't have time to debate with him."

"I understand, and I told him the focus was on John's children. Saving them was the only thing that mattered so he should put his ego aside."

"That must have gone over well."

"No. Actually, he gave me his death look and walked away," the captain said as he erupted in laughter. Ricky joined in and the two continued to bask in their amusement for a while.

The children were released the following day. Doctor Phillips, a child psychiatrist, had talked to each of them and advised immediate therapy for both. Julie took a few recommendations and made a note on her phone to call and set up appointments. John drove them home and Julie cooked a hearty dinner, and the family watched movies together after eating. It grew late, so John said, "It's time to go to bed you two. I'll be up in a minute to say goodnight." They both nodded and headed to their rooms.

He entered Gianna's room first and sat down on the side of her bed.

"I want to tell you something, baby girl. I'm very proud of how you handled yourself and your brother through this. You've matured into a strong young woman before my eyes."

"Thank you, daddy."

"Remember, you'll always be my little girl, and when we're together you can act that way, no matter when or where. You can always come to me to be a child again."

Gianna reached up and hugged her father and John pulled her covers over her shoulder.

"Daddy, why did that man want to hurt us?"

"He wanted to hurt me, and the easiest way to do that was to take you and your brother because he knows how much I love you both."

"So, we didn't do anything wrong?"

"Of course not, baby girl. None of this was your fault. Now get some sleep, I love you."

"I love you too, daddy."

When he entered his son's room, he noticed an odd look on Ryann's face, like he was confused, scared, or both.

"Hi, son. What's on your mind?"

"Hi dad... nothing."

John searched his face and knew something was there, something that he needed to coax out of him.

"Ryann, you can talk to me, maybe I can help."

Ryann looked at his father and John saw a flash of trust cross his face.

"I'm afraid of death."

John put his hand on Ryann's shoulder. "We're all afraid of death. That's nothing to be ashamed of."

"I'm afraid of what it will feel like. What if it's horrible, like being thrown into a pit of fire, or drowning? What if you just can't breathe anymore, like being buried alive?"

"Nature takes care of our pain and suffering. It numbs our senses when something like that happens. I think it's like falling asleep. We fade into a deep dream to live eternity in a pleasant, peaceful place, reunited with the ones we loved in life, like me, mommy, Gianna, Simba..."

"But, how do you know? How do you know it isn't awful?"

"I don't, but it's what I believe. I could be wrong, but probably not," John said as he smiled at his son. "Either way, you have a long life to live before you're going to die, so you need to get some sleep."

John tucked Ryann in and kissed him on the top of his forehead. When he reached the doorway he heard Ryann say, "Thank you, daddy."

"You are welcome," John answered, and shut the door.

John walked into the bedroom and noticed Julie was already asleep. He stepped into the bathroom to wash his face and brush his teeth. He returned to the bedroom, flipped the light off and pulled the covers down, but paused before getting in. He leaned down into the trash bin and picked up the bible he had thrown away. He looked at the cover, then opened it and ran his hand over the smooth pages. He opened the dresser drawer and placed it safely back in its hiding spot, its home. He got in bed, said a short but meaningful prayer, and went to sleep.

For the next few days, John stayed home with his family and they slowly returned to their usual routines of everyday life. They ate together, watched television, played games... whatever they could do together to bring a bit of normal back into their lives. John thought about how strange it was that we complain about the monotony of our boring existence yet yearn for it when it's gone for even the shortest amount of time.

Julie had left with the children to have dinner with Julie's parents. They had invited John, but he took the opportunity to visit the restaurant and talk to Red. He had been holding down the fort without fail and John felt like he should update him on his plan of returning soon. It looked like a slow night as John entered and took his usual spot. John glanced over at an empty bar and wondered where the "Trinity of Jesters" were. It was the first time John could remember not having Sean, Artie, or Matt present.

Tim, a new bartender walked behind the bar and over to John. "Mr. Corbin, I was happy to hear the good news. How are you?"

"I'll be better with a scotch on the rocks and please, Tim, call me John," he said with a small grin.

"Sure thing, coming right up."

Red walked out of the kitchen and immediately spotted his friend. He hurried over and took the seat next to John.

"How is everyone?"

"We're all great, considering. Thanks for asking. How are things here?"

"It's been slow the last few days, but the weekends are packed full."

"Red, I want to thank you for taking this on while I was gone; you're a lifesaver."

"While you were gone? Does that mean you're back?"

"I need a couple more days with my family, then I'll be fully available."

"Welcome back, partner," Red said as he shook John's hand. "We missed ya."

"Thank you. Speaking of missed, where are the clowns?"

Red turned his head to inspect the bar. "Huh, empty. That's a first."

"There goes out liquor sales for the day," John joked.

"Ha, you're not wrong about that. Those boys can drink. So, any more info on who this lunatic is?"

"None. He's very diligent with his crime scenes and communication. We've had our best men on the case and still haven't uncovered one clue. It's infuriating."

"Maybe you should think twice about giving up," Red said.

John quickly turned his head and looked at his friend. "Red, he had my children. I'm by no means giving up. That's the only thing that can make me abandon the case. He didn't win, not this time, but he made the stakes too rich for my blood."

"I understand. But can you let it go? Will it haunt you if you do? The sting will pass, but any more death by his hand will stay with you forever."

John finished off his drink and placed the glass on the bar with a thump. "I need to get back home. Talk soon."

The pair shook hands and John left, passing Sean on his way out.

The following day, John stopped into the station to inform them of his decision. He walked into the captain's office and shut the door behind him. His two colleagues who were in the middle of a heavy conversation with the captain looked up when they heard the door close.

"John! I'm surprised to see you. How's the family?" Captain Johnson said.

"About as well as can be expected. Thankfully, I think we'll all be fine."

Ricky nodded and said seriously, "That's great news, partner. Be diligent with the counseling. Problems may not surface for some time and that experience was as traumatic as it gets."

"I know, that's why I came in today. I won't be coming back. My family needs me now more than ever and I will not put them at further risk. I'm sorry."

Captain Johnson's words were direct and sincere. "John, you have nothing to apologize for. You gave more than could be expected and I thank you for that. If not for hard work and experience, we would have mourned a few more casualties at this point. Right now, your family is more important."

"Thank you. I will forever be in debt to you both. If you need some advice or wisdom going forward, just call or stop by. I'll always be available as a consultant. I just need to step back; I was too close to the flame. My *family* was too close to the flame."

"We understand, and may just take you up on that offer," the captain said.

John shook their hands and walked out of the station, for the second time ending his career doing what he loved.

The dark figure had watched it all unfold: the Corbin children on display fearing for their lives for twenty-four hours, the proceeding rescue... and the love John Corbin displayed for his children. This was fully revealed as he held them on the floor of the tunnel. Although seeing those little necks snap would have been enjoyable and amusing, he could live with the outcome. John was shaken, that was plain to see. He had taken back the power that Mr. Corbin had wrestled from him in the previous rescue. They had played the game by the rules and succeeded. This had all been a means-to-an-end. The final act was still to be played out and the upcoming events would be the climax of his scheme. It would be the equivalent of a beautiful, well planned finale after a long fireworks show. One of the few activities he enjoyed as a child was to sneak out and watch them alone in wonderment of the beauty and power they possessed. His plan contained those very same qualities. Oh yes they did.

The dark figure left his house in the cover of darkness, eager to put the final wheels of his plan in motion.

For the best part was yet to come.

"I hear John is coming back to work," Sean said to Red as he took another gulp of his Brooklyn Summer Ale. Artie arrived and took a seat next to Sean.

"That's the plan, although I have a feeling he may reconsider at some point."

"Why would you say that?"

"I've known John quite a while now. There isn't much we haven't discussed. Let's just say John has the blood of a detective. He can be happy and successful doing whatever he chooses because of his drive and intelligence, but being a cop is in his DNA. That won't just go away."

"He'd be crazy to tempt fate again, not when his family is concerned. I know I would never put my wife at risk. She's my life."

"Yes, we get that from the putrid poems you write," Sean said as he gave Artie a disgusted look.

"Speaking of poems, I have a new one. Want to hear it?"

Red turned and walked out of the bar before Artie could start speaking.

"Dude, I'd rather stick an ice pick in my retina than suffer through another one of your love letters to your wife. Listening to them makes my brain cells want to commit suicide one at a time."

"Well, we all know you need the few hundred you have left, so maybe I'll keep this one to myself," Artie countered, which put a confused look on Sean's face.

"Isn't a couple hundred a lot? I mean, most only have a hundred or so, right?"

Artie looked away in disbelief.

"Ricky, I want you to take the weekend and get away. I know the last abduction has taken its toll on you, as it has all of us. Take Alexis somewhere, reset, clear your mind and enjoy life for a few days. Without John, you'll be my second in command when I'm not present. I need you to be ready to go physically and mentally when this nut strikes again."

"Sir, I don't need—'

Captain Johnson put up his hand to stop Ricky in mid-sentence. "It's an order, not a suggestion."

"Okay, then, I will. Thank you, sir."

After Captain Johnson walked away, Ricky called Alexis.

"Hi, handsome."

"Hi beautiful, how is everything? How's the new book coming?"

"Well, the great part of having my Dad around is we're catching up on lost time, but the bad part is, I have less time to write."

"Well, that's a small price to pay. He needs you now, so make time for him."

"You're right, I shouldn't complain. He fills a void in my life that was always there and I'm always going to be glad for that." She paused a moment, then asked, "How's John, Julie and the children?"

"They're doing well. John resigned. It's going to be difficult to replace his experience and instincts."

"I'm sure, but it was a decision he had to make and I certainly understand."

"Alexis, Captain gave me the weekend off. I would love you to join me."

"Join you where, Mr. Burton?" she asked in a slightly amused tone of voice.

"Willow's Lodge in Woodinville, along the Sammamish River. Rest, relaxation, and a touch of romance to top it off. Some hiking or biking if we get cabin fever, you may even get some writing done."

"Sounds wonderful, but what about the case?"

"Captain thinks I need some time to reset, get my mind right."

"When do we leave, Romeo?"

"Thursday evening."

Alexis didn't even hesitate. "It's a date."

On Friday, late in the afternoon, Captain Johnson stood in front of the station and updated the media on The Seattle Slayer case. When he finished, he agreed to answer some questions.

"Captain Johnson, do you have any leads at all concerning the identification of The Seattle Slayer?" asked Nicole Kearns from the Seattle Times.

"No, not at this time, Nicole. As soon as I do, you will be the first to know."

"Why did he target the Corbin children?" asked John Bryant from KOMO 4 news.

"At this point, we don't know why the Corbin children were targeted."

"There are reports that he plays games with your force, sends puzzles you need to solve to find his current victim. Can you confirm this, and if this is so, why?" This question came from an anonymous source.

"This man is a narcissist who likes to flaunt his intelligence and challenge us to beat him at his own game. These puzzles bolster his ego and opinion of himself. He's a very dangerous man with sociopathic tendencies."

"Sorry sir, but is it confirmed that the murderer is a he? Is it possible it could be a woman?" asked an anonymous female.

"We have reasons to believe it is a man, although we haven't confirmed this."

"Then shouldn't you state the fact that it could be a female?"

"No, as I've stated, we believe it to be a male. Folks, every moment lost is a moment his next victim is closer to death. Do you think I care about or have time for political correctness? I will wrap this up for now. Good day."

Captain Johnson walked inside the station, into his office and closed the door behind him. Minutes later he noticed a new email...

Michael, that's not like you to lose your cool. Have I gotten under your skin? Surely you can handle a little question about my gender better than that...

The captain closed the email, threw a pen across his office and it exploded against the far wall. He got up, shut the light, and headed out the door after informing everyone he was leaving for the night. It was a long week and he needed a break from the craziness. He needed a night home with his wife. He walked out into a warm summer night with a bright moon shining from high in the Seattle sky.

Ricky watched Alexis step out of the shower and smile at him moments before grabbing a towel to cover up. They had just completed another intense session of lovemaking and Ricky was reveling in the aftermath. He could not remember a time in his life when he was happier. The weekend was coming to an end, they would drive back home later this evening and resume their typical schedules and lives in the morning, but they both had some wonderful memories of their time spent together. Ricky grabbed a bottle of red wine with two glasses and headed for their secluded patio overlooking an herb garden and terrace.

"Meet me outside after you dry off," he said as he opened the French doors and stepped out.

Moments later she appeared wearing tight athletic shorts enhancing her lovely curves and a white tee-shirt revealing the roundness of her ample breasts, as the moonlight shone down on her.

"It's beautiful," she said as she glanced up at the clear sky displaying a bright half-moon and vivid stars.

Ricky smiled and followed her gaze to the heavens. "There are certain times I become angry about life. I analyze, study, work... all in hope of making the correct decision to be successful at whatever I'm trying to accomplish. When I feel I've done that, worked the percentages in my favor and yet still fail, I feel cheated. Especially when I observe some lazy, incompetent slob achieve the goal from pure luck. But you know what I think of in those moments?"

"You think about this wonderful, caring woman who has just recently entered your life?"

Ricky glanced at Alexis and smirked. "Yes, but when I'm done thinking about her, I think about this." He waved his arm at the sky, at the moon, at the stars. "This image brings me perspective. It makes all the petty issues in life that we call problems that we stress over seem insignificant. It makes me just happy to be alive."

Alexis walked to Ricky and put her arms around him, and together they gazed at the wonder and beauty of the world.

"It's amazing, to think how big the universe is. You're right, it makes us feel minute and unimportant. Do you think there are other forms of life out there?"

"Of course. I mean, it would be naïve and myopic to think otherwise. There are millions of solar systems out there, many with environments that may support life. It's fascinating to think about all the different species and life forms that may be out there right now, thinking about whether *we* exist or not, a billion light years away."

"To think, all those stars, planets and solar systems and you found me right here, in the same town. Do you believe in fate or destiny, that things happen for a reason?"

"No. I believe I met you because some lunatic happened to kidnap your father and it's my job to save him. It just so happens that those beautiful eyes got my attention."

"You definitely need to read some romance novels. Your perception of love at first sight is pretty dry."

Ricky laughed and grabbed Alexis by the waist, placed her on the floor of the patio and made love to her again, deep into the night, under the watch of a million stars.

John returned to the restaurant the following week and invited the captain and Ricky in for lunch. Red joined the trio, and talk soon returned to the Seattle Slayer.

"Anything new?" John asked.

"Nope. No videos, no new evidence; he seems to be taking his time," Captain Johnson replied.

"Maybe he'll just go away," Red said.

"A pleasant thought, but not likely. He seems to have a reason to continue. Many serial killers can have bursts of activity then become benign for long periods of time. Others become addicted and can't get enough, almost like drug addicts. Those are killers who kill for sport, just for the experience. I think our guy has a plan that he intends to pursue to its entirety," Ricky said.

"What makes you think that?" Red asked.

John leaned forward. "Ricky's right, if he just wanted to kill, he would do just that. He wants to prove and accomplish something, thus the puzzles,"

The food arrived, and the subject changed to family, friends, and talk of the Mariners winning the American League West. After dessert, Ricky and Captain Johnson got up to leave. John walked them out.

"Let me know as soon as you hear anything."

"We will. Take care, John. Tell Julie and the kids we were asking for them."

John watches as his colleagues drove away, part of him yearning to be with them. John pushed that feeling away and buried it deep inside and went back into his restaurant.

The dark figure had been watching his next victim for days, learning its schedule, noticing the gaps of vulnerability in its days. He learned its size and weight to the exact pound, to make sure to use the exact amount of Succinylcholine. As his next victim slowly crawled away from him with a tranquilizer dart secured in the middle of its back, the dark figure felt a feeling of pride for a job well done. The victim stopped crawling and grew faint, finally turned to look at its assailant. The last sight that seared into the victim's mind was of the dark figure approaching, with a disturbing, victorious smile on his face.

CHAPTER EIGHT

24:00:00, 23:59:59, 23:59:58...

The victim's eyes slowly opened, the heavy grogginess from the Succinylcholine dart slowly fading. When clear vision returned, complete panic and terror reigned. The victim was erected on a cross, with each limb secured by a cable to a pulley. Each pulley was then connected to one master pulley which was connected to a pressure plate. Hanging above the pressure plate was a palette of bricks suspended by a hefty rope. The bricks were to be used as a counterweight and when released, would depress the plate and activate the pulleys. The victim understood immediately what the purpose of the setup conveyed — dismemberment. The cross itself was suspended above the ground and constructed then attached to two huge trees. The victim glanced around at the surroundings. The site was a thick forest with the glow of moonlight cascading through the treetops. The dark figure stood behind the camera and smiled, noticing the moment the victim recognized the meaning of the whole mechanism.

"Nice of you to finally join me, I've been lonely. You could try to scream, but I assure you, nobody would hear you out here," the dark figure said. "Time to get down to business, I'm sure everyone's been waiting for the show to start."

23:35:03, 23:35:02, 23:35:01...

Ricky sat at his desk finishing up some paperwork before heading home for the evening. He placed the last document in a file, then turned his attention toward his computer and noticed an email from an unnamed source. He reached for his mouse to open it as Rosalie called over his phone.

"Ricky, I have Mrs. Johnson on line one for you."

"Okay, thank you, Rosalie." He picked up his phone and pressed line one.

"Hello, Mrs. Johnson, what can I help you with?"

"Hi Ricky, do you know what time Michael left the station today? He still isn't home. The last time we talked he said he would be home for dinner and that was hours ago."

"Really? He left late this afternoon right before sunset. You haven't spoken to him since?"

"No, he usually comes straight home. I called him on his cell but got his voicemail. Please ask around and call me if you hear anything."

"Sure, will do, Mrs. Johnson."

"Ricky, you know you can call me Sarah."

"I know, but I'm an old-fashioned boy. I'll call as soon as I hear anything."

"Thank you."

Ricky placed the phone back down and hesitated for a moment. A look of recollection combined with terror suddenly came over his face. He clicked on the email...

Good evening detective Burton. AND THEN THERE WAS ONE! I hate to break up our little group, we were having so much fun, but

it needed to be done. A means to an end and all. I'm sure you will forgive me.

Under the text, there was a link to another video. Ricky clicked on the link.

There, nailed to a cross like Jesus Christ himself, was Captain Johnson.

23:01:03, 23:01:02, 23:01:01...

John was at the restaurant when he received a text from Ricky:

Forwarded you an email I need you to see

John quickly went to his office, closed the door, and opened his email. He clicked on the link and when the video feed loaded, he stared at the screen in horror. "No..."

He immediately called Ricky's cell.

"John, I—"

"Ricky, who knows?" John said, cutting Ricky off.

"Me, you, Rosalie, the feds, Detective Bernard and Sarah—"

"Sarah knows?"

"Yes, Sarah knows. She called me looking for the captain hours earlier. I had to call and inform her. She's obviously distraught. Listen, John, I didn't send the feed to you to change your mind or involve you, I just thought you should know."

"Of course. Do we have any information?"

"No, nothing yet." Ricky paused, secretly hoping John would tell him to hold tight, that he was on his way in, and that they would work the case together. Part of him knew that was selfish and knew John was better off uninvolved.

"How and when was he abducted?"

"We don't know for certain yet, but it seems like it happened between four and five hours ago."

"Please let me know as soon as any info becomes available."

"Will do, I'll be in touch."

John disconnected the call and threw his head back. He felt the tension in the base of his skull, the queasiness in his stomach, and his heartbeat quicken as he closed his eyes and put his hands over his face.

22:39:03, 22:39:02, 23:39:01...

Michael Johnson frantically studied the landscape around him for a clue as to his whereabouts but all he could see were trees of all shapes and sizes in every direction. He noticed many Douglas-firs, Sitka spruce, western hemlock, and even some giant western red cedar. The state of Washington contained many forests, however. Looking at the size and density of the trees, he knew he had to be in the middle of one of the more extensive forests the state had to offer. *Must be near Mt. Rainer, North Cascades, the Wenatchee Forest, or Olympic Forest,* he thought. He then noticed the growth of moss on the trunks of many trees and branches. The thickness of the moss combined with the size of the trees left no doubt; he was somewhere in the middle of the Olympic National Forest. Realizing he was totally alone, he tried to loosen his restraints, starting with his hands, but they were expertly fastened. There was no way he could free himself. He found his feet to be just as secured as he tried to kick them back and forth to cause some slack, but there was no give. He settled down and leaned his head back against the top of the cross and looked directly into the camera. *All the time I have spent fighting crime, and I have never been on this side,* he thought. *It feels surreal, almost like I am living in a horror movie.*

Clouds moved slowly in covering the moon for periods as the forest turned even darker. He heard some movement in the bush to his left and heard the low, deep grunt of a black bear. For the first time, he was glad he was ten feet off the ground. A storm cloud opened up, sending a symphony of raindrops through the trees.

22:21:03, 22:21:02, 22:21:01...

John left the restaurant with a tension headache brewing at the base of his skull. He arrived at a quiet house with the children already asleep in their beds. Julie was also asleep with an open book sprawled on her chest. John carefully picked the book up, slid the bookmark inside, and placed it on the nightstand. John walked into the bathroom, shut the door quietly and studied his reflection in the mirror. His thoughts returned to an evening almost thirty years ago.

July 22, 1988. Seattle, Washington...

John Corbin was a rookie cop on the Seattle Police force. He had responded to a call about a disturbance on his beat. Unbeknownst to John, someone had taken a young woman hostage in an apartment complex on the top floor. John walked up to room 412 and knocked on the door. "Help!" he heard followed by a muffled smack and, "Shut up bitch!" John pulled his gun and kicked in the door. He saw, straight through the living room on the balcony, a silhouette of a man holding a woman at gunpoint. John quickly moved behind a wall.

"Drop the gun!" John yelled.

"I'm going to kill this bitch and then jump! Leave, pig!" This was the first situation that John had encountered which was more serious than the usual traffic violation or minor domestic disturbance. He had been on the beat for only a month, and now he was being thrown straight into the fire. John called it in. Dispatch informed him that backup including Detective Johnson was on his way, but John didn't think he could wait. This man was dangerous and on edge.

"Sir, please let the girl go. You and I can handle this."

"Why would I do that? I want to send a message to all the people that disrespected me, laughed at me, and treated me like shit. Taking her with me will do just that!"

"Let her go and take me instead. What better way to make a statement than to take out a cop? I'm putting my gun down. Let her go, and I will come forward to you."

John was surprised to find the perp accept his offer. He let the girl go, and John took her place. He pulled John to the edge of the balcony to the increasing gasps of the growing crowd that had formed below.

"I have to give you credit copper, you got guts," the man said as he put the gun to John's head. "But why? Why would you give your life for another?"

"Reasons I'm sure you would never understand. It's my duty and who I am," The perp gave a little sly grin, like he thought John an idiot and pushed the gun against his temple. A shot rang out into the warm, humid, summer Seattle air. John opened his eyes and was shocked to discover he was still alive. The perp had fallen on the balcony with a lone gunshot wound through his head. John turned and saw Detective Johnson lowering his weapon.

"Damn rookie, you've got a pair of brass balls. You saved her life, son. Good work."

"Yeah, and you saved mine," John breathed.

"Maybe, but what you just did is the kind of thing that gets remembered on this force. I won't forget it."

Detective Johnson would become captain within three years.

21:38:03, 21:38:02, 21:38:01...

Ricky made his way into the feds office to speak with Agent Daniels. Since Ricky's little maneuver in the tunnel, Daniels had been working on reigning the young detective in. Ricky knew without the captain here to run the show and filter him from the feds, he was now open game. He walked in and sat across the desk from Daniels who got up, shut the door and sat back down.

"Detective Burton, now that Mr. Johnson is currently unavailable, I will assume full control of this investigation. Another stunt like the last one you pulled, and I will suspend you, understood?"

"Yes," Ricky answered to the icy stare of his superior.

"Anything you hear, see, feel, or think about this case will be forwarded to me. We have two homicides, five abductions already, and a good man's life hangs in the balance. I don't want this video feed in anybody's hands but who I approve beforehand. We need to work together in an orderly, structured pattern. Your rogue, cowboy bullshit will not work and will not be tolerated. Again, do you understand?"

"Absolutely, sir."

Daniels looked at him with the coldest, untrusting stare Ricky had ever seen or felt, but he kept his head high and matched the agent's cold gaze with his own.

"That will be all."

Ricky got up, opened the door and took one step out before Daniels called to him.

"Oh, and Burton…"

Ricky turned around with a guarded look.

"I'm watching you."

Ricky shut the door and walked away.

19:35:03, 19:35:02, 19:35:01…

Somehow, in just under four and a half hours the press got wind of the captain's abduction. Ricky believed there was a leak somewhere in the dozen federal agents now assigned to the case. The national news has shown up and demanded a presser. The case had grown nationally to gigantic proportions, as a couple of prime-time news programs were in town to dedicate full shows on "The Seattle Slayer." Agent Daniels set up a conference in front of the station to answer questions.

"Agent Daniels, is it true Captain Michael Johnson has been abducted?"

"At this time, we cannot confirm that."

"Is Detective Corbin still involved?"

"No, Detective Corbin is on leave from the force."

"Do you have any more info on who The Seattle Slayer is and what he wants?"

"I cannot share any info on our subject at this time. He is a very disturbed individual who needs to be apprehended and brought to justice."

"Do you have a profile you are working off of?"

"Yes. Caucasian male, twenty-five to forty-five, extremely unstable and extremely dangerous. Now, ladies and gentlemen, I have an investigation to lead. Good day."

Daniels walked away from the cameras and microphones and back into the station. He gave Ricky another wintry look as he passed, then entered his office, concluding the whole spectacle with a violent slam of the door.

18:10:03, 18:10:02, 18:10:01...

John lay in bed with a motley cluster of thoughts racing through his head. He imagined his comrade and good friend alone, waiting to die. He glanced over at Julie who was resting comfortably in a deep sleep. He got up and headed downstairs to pour himself a glass of scotch. He settled on the sofa with his drink in front of him, set his head back, and recalled a moment long ago...

January 4, 1990. Seattle, Washington...

John Corbin walked into Captain Johnson's office and stood in front of his desk. Michael Johnson had received a well-earned promotion from detective to captain on December 17^h; he then spent the following two weeks adjusting his police force to fit his needs.

"Officer Corbin... John, sit down."

"Thank you, sir."

The captain wasted no time on ceremony. "I am going to promote you to detective effective immediately. I've watched you and witnessed an officer dedicated to his service of his civilians, a man driven to find the truth, and have justice served. I believe in my instincts, and they tell me you're ready for the next challenge in your career. I believe this city would benefit and this force would benefit with you having more responsibility, free to use your intelligence and drive to solve cases instead of chasing criminals on the streets."

"Thank you, captain."

"Of course, the promotion comes with a package including a salary raise and a slew of additional benefits that I would be happy to go over with you. Do you accept my offer?"

"I do, it's what I've wanted from my first day. Thank you, captain."

"You earned it, son. Welcome aboard."

John held his glass up to the light and admired the golden, amber hue of the scotch, then finished it off before pouring another.

17:47:03, 17:47:02, 17:47:01...

Ricky glanced through the front windows as a mob of journalists, reporters, columnists, and civilians gathered, waiting to ask questions. With the rumors of the captain's abduction, the case of The Seattle Slayer had risen to enormous proportions and members of the press were eager to ask questions of anyone who may have any inside information on the case. Ricky noticed Daniels had no intention of appeasing the press and making another appearance until he had no choice. Ricky disliked Daniels and his heavy-handed way of running things. Captain Johnson was more liberal, more democratic; and although some may think that would cause him to obtain less from his workers, his methods worked very well. There is something to be said for letting people breathe and use their own intelligence and instincts, and Captain Johnson had mastered that balance. Ricky already missed him. Not only as a boss, but also as a life mentor and father figure. He knew without Captain Johnson's leadership and John's experience and intuition, the chances of rescuing him were slim. Ricky checked the video feed and watched as rain continued to fall on the lonesome man whose head was as erect and alert as ever. *He will never give up, he doesn't know how to,* Ricky thought, as he heard the rain start to fall outside the Seattle Police Department Headquarters. *If it has been raining in the video for four hours, he must be being held west of here. The storm clouds are slow moving and heading east. He must be in the Olympic Forest. The problem is the Olympic Forest is huge, almost fifteen hundred square miles.*

He noticed something else from the feed; there was no sound of the rain hitting the leaves and ground. The killer had turned it off. All the others had sound. He reasoned to himself that it was to ensure no communication from the captain in any way through the video. Ricky stood and headed for Daniel's office to fill him in on his thoughts.

17:01:03, 17:01:02, 17:01:01...

Michael felt the showers slow to a stop as the clouds moved east. He was sheltered from most of the rain by the heavy tree cover but he was wet and could feel some water trickle down his face and neck. *How we take for granted the use of our limbs until it's gone,* he thought, as the desire to wipe the rivulets of water became obsessive. *So, this is what water torture feels like.*

A soft breeze kicked up out of the west and the scent of pine and fresh rain filled his nasal passages. For a moment he felt free, with nothing but the sights, sounds, and aromas of nature saturating his senses.

16:30:03, 16:30:02, 16:30:01...

John didn't sleep. He sat on the sofa, nursing another scotch and watching the national news station air a quick report on the rumors that The Seattle Slayer had abducted Michael Johnson, the Seattle Police Captain. The report mentioned how John and his children, along with Brain Simmons, had survived their abductions. The report concluded by mentioning the case was now being run by Agent Daniels, and the hope was he would apprehend the killer. John closed his eyes and thought of another memory.

November 13, 2014...

"Last night I strangled Silas Alvah to death. He killed Todd, Jacqueline, and their unborn child. He was there the night they died. I have proof of this on Todd's cell phone. He confessed to me that he did it right before I ended his life. I wanted to keep innocent people safely out of his reach, and this was the only way to do that without the risk of him getting free again. I wanted to bring him to justice, to give his victims the revenge they all deserved. Sir, I don't know if it was the right thing to do, but sitting here now, I wouldn't change it. I would do it all again. If I need to pay for what I've done, so be it. But I'd do it all again, exactly the same way."

The captain sat there and looked at John for what seemed to be an eternity. He then got up, paced the room, then sat back down across from John, still speechless. Finally, he got up and walked out without uttering a word. John assumed that a few of his brethren, his brothers, would be in to arrest him and take him away. John waited. No arrest came. No captain. Nothing.

Finally, the door opened, and the captain walked back in and sat down.

"Although I feel your actions were wrong and you have lost your way as a detective and a cop, I'm keeping this between you and me. I know what you're made of. You are a hero. From the first time I saw you put your life on the line to save an innocent woman, I knew it. I can't arrest you. I won't let them arrest you and convict you. In the structure of the law, what you did was a crime, but somewhere deep inside my soul, what you did gives me a bright, healthy feeling. Hell, maybe I've been doing this too long as well. I will cover up the Silas Alvah killing. This is my decision, not yours. It's over."

"Sir, I don't know if that is the correct way to handle this," John had said.

"Do you ever want to see your children again? They need you. It's over. My decision is made. This world is a better place with you in it. This world is a better place with you in it as a free man. It's over."

John brought his hands to his face as the memories occupied his mind. Captain Johnson time and again stood by him and stuck his neck out because he believed in the person John was. It was hard to forget that now, even with his family involved.

15:05:03, 15:05:02, 15:05:01...

"Agent Daniels, I believe Captain Johnson is being held in the Olympic Forest," Ricky said as he sat in front of Agent Daniel's desk.

"Why do you think that, Burton?"

"I studied the weather pattern, along with the types and volume of the trees in the video."

"Burton, when are weather patterns consistent enough to use as evidence? Also, if I'm not mistaken, that type of flora is found all over Washington State, is it not?"

"It is, just not in that size or density. It's a gut feeling, sir, an instinct."

"Burton, we don't base investigations on gut feelings; you should know better than that."

"At one time, I would have agreed with you, but someone I respect very much has taught me otherwise."

"Even if this improbable idea is correct, do you realize how big the Olympic Forest is? That search would take days, if not weeks. We have just over fifteen hours."

"I know. We need to narrow it down somehow. I just wanted to pass my theory on to you," Ricky said as he rose to leave Agent Daniel's office.

"Burton, if you can expand on your theory or your gut instinct, be sure to fill me in."

"Will do, sir," Ricky answered before walking out.

13:48:03, 13:48:02, 13:48:01...

The ringtone of John's cell chimed. He picked it up and hit the green button to answer even though he had no recollection of the number.

"Hello?"

"John? This is Sarah Johnson."

John immediately sat up. "Hi Mrs. Johnson, I'm so sorry—"

"Thank you," she said, cutting him off before he could finish. "John, I am not calling you to ask you to save my husband. Michael told me your reasons for leaving the case and I understand perfectly well that you had to do it. Family is the most important thing in this world, and you need to protect yours at all costs."

"Thank you, ma'am."

"Having said that, you know Michael means the world to me and I would very much appreciate if you could relay to me any information you discover about him. Detective Burton hasn't said much, and I believe Agent Daniels has muzzled the entire force. I don't like that man one bit."

"Sarah, I'll fill you in on anything I can find out. I know I don't have to tell you how close I am to your husband. He's my mentor and older brother. I owe everything to him."

"He speaks very highly of you, John. He always had from your first week on the force, years ago." John could hear muffled sobs and at that moment he closed his eyes and prayed for the safety of his boss. "I just can't imagine life without him. I'm sorry." She was crying freely now.

"No need to be sorry, I understand. I'll do everything I can to help him."

"I need to go now but thank you for listening."

She hung up and John looked at his phone as the line disconnected. He placed it down and lay back as the soothing effects of the scotch numbed his grief. He knew Sarah would never call him to persuade him to get involved. He believed her when she said she understood and respected his decision. However, he felt guilt when he thought about her husband and his friend whose life was being held captive in the hands of a ruthless killer.

12:00:03, 12:00:02, 12:00:01…

Ricky waited for a message containing the clue that would hopefully lead them to Captain Johnson. He watched the screen in anticipation, but nothing came. He checked the time counting down on the video feed: 11:58:03.

Is it just late? he wondered, although the un-sub had been meticulously punctual. Something was definitely off. He then went into his own email and there was a new message from an unknown source. He eagerly opened it:

Hi again, Detective Burton. I'm sure you are wondering why I have changed the usual protocol and sent this directly to you. I have a plan and I know Daniels would have interfered with it once he saw my demands. This is what I want and what you will do if you ever want to see your beloved chief again.

Do not relay this message to Daniels. I want John Corbin, and John Corbin alone to meet me at a specified place. From there I will take him to where I am holding Michael. Yes, I call him Michael now. We have had some time to bond and really have become good friends! But I digress.

If John follows my rules I will free your chief. If anyone follows, I will know. To attempt to go off script will cost Mr. Johnson his life, and probably John's as well, so I cannot stress this enough: HE MUST COME ALONE. If you refuse these demands, I will end Michael's life. This all must be kept between us three: me, you and Mr. Corbin.

Failure to do so will cause undue pain to Michael, and I really do not want to see him go through that.

Ricky reread the message a few times to make sure he understood every detail.

"Burton, any message?" Daniels asked from behind him. Ricky frantically minimized the message into his tray.

"No sir, he seems to have gone off structure. Maybe he's evolving; changing his routine."

Ricky felt Daniels search his face for any sign of deceit. *This guy doesn't trust anyone,* he thought, as he did his best to look Daniels in the eyes with a cold, hard stare.

"Okay, well, let me know if anything changes."

"Will do, sir."

With that, Daniels was gone and Ricky was left alone to determine how he should handle the situation. After evaluating his position, he forwarded the email to John and sent him a text:

John, I'm sorry to bring you back into this, but I thought you would want to know. I forwarded you an email from our killer. He only wants you and me to know.

Ricky leaned back in his chair and put his hands on his head. He didn't like this one bit, but he had no power. They were all at the mercy of this lunatic if they ever wanted to see the captain alive again. He felt the tension build in his neck and a steady ache began to throb in his temples.

11:45:03, 11:45:02, 11:45:01...

John put the scotch away. Drinking himself to oblivion wouldn't help the situation at all and he needed to keep a somewhat clear head in case he was called upon for support. As he reached for the remote to change the television station, he heard his text tone on his phone go off. He picked up his phone and opened the text from Ricky. He typed in a response:

I'll check the email now

John grabbed his laptop from the kitchen counter and opened his email. After reading the killer's demands, John closed his eyes and threw his head back against the couch cushion. At first, he would not accept the situation. He kept coming up with scenarios that would save the captain without his involvement. After exhausting his mind John thought about Sarah. He could sense the pain she felt over the phone. He heard her pleading tone, felt her frantic agony. Sarah Johnson wasn't a woman who was ever pleading or frantic, but that was with Michael in her life. John knew what he had to do. There was no other choice he could make. He couldn't sit back and let Captain Johnson die. He would meet with Ricky and devise a plan. For the second time in six months, John Corbin would come out of retirement.

11:01:03, 11:01:02, 11:01:01...

Ricky felt his cell vibrate in his pocket as he waited for another email from the killer. He was starting to feel every second tick away, knowing with each moment that passes the chances of finding and saving the captain declined. He took out the phone and saw a notification of a new text:

Ricky, I'm in. We will have to meet in my office at the restaurant when you receive the next email. Forward whatever he sends you. I'll be in touch.

Ricky put his phone away and checked his email. Nothing. He thought about a famous quote he heard a few times.
Patience is not the ability to wait, but the ability to keep a good attitude while waiting...

"Fuck that," he said out loud as a fed walked by and looked at him like he had three eyes. He waved and shook his head, pretending he was reading a disturbing article online.

10:45:03, 10:45:02, 10:45:01...

John slowly made his trek upstairs to inform Julie of his intent. He dreaded having this conversation with his wife for two reasons: The first was that he knew it would frighten her and cause her much stress. The second was that she was absolutely right, he shouldn't do this. John knew he may not ever come home.

He entered the bedroom and sat on the bed next to Julie, who woke instantly. She knew, just by the look in his eyes, she knew. He could never hide emotions from her; his soul was permanently nude in front of her.

"John, no."

He dropped his eyes in shame. "I have too. He is going to kill Michael if I don't go."

Julie jumped up and grabbed John by the arm. "Follow me," she said and led him into Ryann's room. "That is your son." She then pulled him into Gianna's room. "That is your daughter. Look at her. Do you ever want to see her again? Do you want to see your children graduate school, go to college, get married, have children of their own?"

"Of course I—"

"Then stay here. Do not go. John, you won't make it back. You can't leave us."

John walked back into the bedroom and sat on his side of the bed. Julie followed right behind him. He rubbed the top of his head with his hand and looked up at his wife, who he loved intensely.

"This is what I am, Julie. This is what you married. I'm a cop. I will always be a cop. Sure, I can pretend to be a restaurant owner, maybe even find something else to occupy my time for a few years. But ultimately, I will always come back to being a cop, and cops save people. That is what I was put on this earth for."

"You can't save everyone, John, no matter how hard you try. There will always be more who die, whether you're a cop or not. You need to move on. Your children need you. *I* need you!"

John dropped his head. "I'm sorry... I have to do this."

Julie walked into the bathroom and locked the door behind her.

Before leaving, John wrote "I LOVE YOU ALL" on a piece of paper and left it on the counter. He petted Simba who looked up at him with eyes filled with sorrow, as if the Malamute knew the stakes in this game. John gave his dog one last pet on the top of his head and walked out.

10:38:03, 10:38:02, 10:38:01...

The email finally appeared. Ricky opened it and read:

In four hours from now, John Corbin will meet me at a small dock on Pine Lake in Olympic Forest. He will come alone, or I will kill your captain, no questions asked. I will know if he is unaccompanied or not and if you think otherwise, try me. From the lake, I will escort Detective Corbin to where Michael is being held. There we will all work out our differences. If everyone does as I say, we all may live.

Ricky forwarded the message to John, the whole time keeping an eye out for Daniels and his cronies.

10:28:03, 10:28:02, 10:28:01...

On the way to the restaurant, John dialed Mrs. Johnson's number.

"Hello?"

"Hi Sarah, I'm going to him. I will do everything I can to save him."

"John, I didn't want you to get involved in this way. Where is he? How do you know you will be safe?"

"We never do know that. Surely you understand that as much as anyone. This is part of the deal; true cops accept the dangers. That's what we sign up for when we put our signatures on the contract. I have to go now, I'll update you as soon as I can."

"John, please be careful."

"I will."

John pulled into the lot and parked. Before going in, he checked his phone for any messages and saw a new email from Ricky. He opened it up and absorbed it. He put his head back and contemplated the situation. Moments later he sent a text to Ricky:

At the restaurant, meet me here asap

He put his phone away and headed inside.

10:15:03, 10:15:02, 10:15:01...

Julie heard John leave and she now had to face the reality that she may never see him again. A large part of being a cop's wife is accepting the fact that any night he may not come home alive. This case obviously carried much more risk, as Captain Johnson was being used as bait to get to John. Was the lunatic's end game to kill her husband? She buried her face in her hands and wept. How would she tell her children? How would she live without him? She hated him for his decision, but in an ironic, twisted contradiction, she loved him because of it, as well. The man she fell in love with is the man who would put his life on the line to save someone else. He was correct, she knew who he was when she married him. She had to accept that now, just as she always has. We can't change the flames that ignite our souls. We can't change who we are or what our passions burn for. She married a cop, she married a hero and that is exactly what she got.

10:02:03, 10:02:02, 10:02:01...

Ricky walked into John's office and sat down across the desk from his partner.

"I'm going, Ricky. I'll drive myself out there and meet that son of a bitch. You go back to the station and keep Daniels off guard until the five-hour mark. Tell him what is going down and send out a party for us. By then I'll have gotten to the bottom of what this psycho wants.

"John, are you sure this is the right decision?"

"No, of course not, but this is the only way we may save the captain."

Ricky shook his head and looked away.

"Hey, don't do that. Don't for a second hold yourself responsible for whatever happens. You did the right thing. If he had asked for you, you would have gone. That's what we do. That's who we are."

"I know."

"Now, go back to the station and keep that dickhead busy until I can do what needs to be done."

Ricky stood up and John shook his hand and patted him on the shoulder. Ricky turned and walked out without looking back.

9:30:03, 9:30:02, 9:30:01...

John headed west on Interstate 5 South. It would be a three-hour drive to arrive at his destination, and he planned to use the long ride to organize his thoughts and play out every scenario in his head. The problem was, he didn't understand the killer's motive, so any scenario he created would be based on a false, crumbling foundation. This would be a purely reactionary situation, which meant he needed to be ready for anything. He had one of his guns in the glove compartment, but he couldn't kill this nut-job until he knew the captain was safe. The killer might have rigged a fail-safe method to kill Johnson if he himself died. He also knew he wouldn't be able to sneak it past the killer. He was going in bare. The killer would have all the power and leverage and John knew for both he and Captain Johnson to both make it through this alive, he needed to handle the situation perfectly. But even then it may not matter.

John Corbin may already be a dead-man.

8:23:03, 8:23:02, 8:23:01…

"Burton, where the fuck have you been?" Daniels yelled as Ricky walked into the station.

"Sorry, sir. I got tied up."

"Tied up doing what? Please don't let us interrupt your personal life, it's only your captain's life at stake here. Have you received any new info? We have yet to obtain any emails. This is a major breakdown in his M.O."

"Nothing has come, sir."

"I had my men study the weather pattern and I think you may have been onto something with your Olympic Forest theory. It will be like finding a needle in a haystack, but I have no other statistical analysis or data to follow. I'm sending four search parties out there… copters, snipers, the whole nine yards."

"Good call, sir." Ricky knew that the copters would get to the region much quicker than John. He just hoped they would search the wrong areas. Daniels' men could ruin the whole operation if they find the killer, and that would be the end for Captain Johnson.

7:48:03, 7:48:02, 7:48:01…

Agent Phillips led a search team over the Olympic Forest. The powerful spotlight illuminated the dense woods below, but he couldn't make out anything that looked anomalous. His copter was responsible for the southern section and the other two the central and northern. His directive was to search until he found the victim or the eight hours remaining ran out, whichever came first. He detested failing and incompetence, so he was determined to find their man. However, success in this mission would require an unusual amount of luck. Brian Phillips was not a man who liked to rely on luck in anything in life. In a frustrated mood, he called back to base.

"Agent Daniels, sir, I have nothing yet, over."

"Keep looking, Phillips."

"Will do, sir," he answered. With the wave of his hand, he motioned for the pilot to start another pass. As the moon starting to break out from behind the clouds, the pair knew they had a long night ahead of them.

6:25:03, 6:25:02, 6:25:01...

John turned onto NF-2370 and drove the two and a half miles until he reached Pine Lake. He parked his truck on the side of the road and walked south around the edge of the pond. The darkness engulfed him as he made his way, carefully measuring each step, as a twisted ankle or knee wouldn't serve him well. He reached the southernmost point and turned north, keeping his eyes open for a dock. His blood hammered through his veins with every step and his senses were on high alert. He heard something scurry through the brush to the left and he turned, expecting to be greeted by The Seattle Slayer himself. Whatever it was hurried away, obviously frightened by the large human invading its territory.

Next time it may be something bigger he thought, as he noticed an opening in the shrubbery straight ahead. He quickened his pace and found himself standing on an overgrown path leading to the water's edge. He followed it out, his eyes opened wide taking in every detail in case he needed to communicate his location in the future. The dock came into sight; a small wooden jetty painted white. He stepped onto the plank and immediately felt the barrel of a gun in his back.

"Hi there, John Corbin, it's a pleasure to finally meet the legend."

"Who are you?" John said as the man patted him down.

"In time, Johnny boy, in time. First you need to go save your captain."

6:12:03, 6:12:02, 6:12:01...

"Who the fuck are you?"

"Keep walking, straight ahead," the man replied as he pushed the tip of his gun deeper into John's back.

The moon's glowing rays shone down which brightened the terrain enough for John to see directly in front of him. Strangely, John's mind wandered to the moon as he glanced up and watched the branches of the thick canopy pass through the brightness. He remembered reading somewhere that the moon glowed simply because the sun's rays reflected off its surface. *Strange the thoughts that take over our minds in times of crisis and strife* he thought as an opening appeared ahead.

As they came upon the break in the brush, John thought he heard the faint hum of a copter in the distance. He stopped in the center of the small clearing. Straight ahead, nailed to a cross and suspended off the ground, was Captain Johnson.

5:58:03, 5:58:02, 5:58:01...

"Captain, are you alr—"

John felt the butt of the gun connect to the back of his head and he went down face first. He felt a trickle of blood flow through his hair and dizziness overtook him, but he remained coherent.

On his knees from the blow, he said, "Okay, I did what you wanted. Let him go and tell me what this is about."

"Oh, no, your chief will not be leaving us just yet, Mr. Corbin. He is my collateral. You obviously were stupid enough to come here to save him, so I will keep him around for a bit longer."

Even engulfed in darkness, in one of the densest forests in North America, John could see the man's grotesque smile. A vision popped into his mind of his hands around the man's throat, squeezing the life out of him.

"My name is Gabriel Crimson. I believe you knew one of my relatives. I didn't know I had a half-brother until he tracked me down. I was euphoric. You see, I didn't have much of a family. My father was a priest, but I never knew him. He impregnated my mother who spent every Sunday worshipping God in his church. She gave me up for adoption and I was abused, physically, emotionally, and sexually by my foster father. It went on for years, but I finally broke free of him and lived my own life. But, I never had a family, a *real* family, until my half-brother came into my life. My mother's name was Tracy. Tracy Alvah. Her other son was named Silas. Silas Alvah was my brother, the brother you took from me."

5:32:03, 5:32:02, 5:32:01…

Captain Johnson, who had been quietly taking it all in, suddenly understood everything.

"John, get out of here. Run…"

Gabriel Crimson turned to the captain and screamed, *"You shut the fuck up! You let him get away with murdering my brother! You let him off free, without paying at all for what he did!"*

"Your brother was a murdering psychopath. He deserved what John did to him," The captain growled in response.

"That wasn't for either of you to decide! Now you both will pay for your sins, just the way my brother did!"

Gabriel walked over to the counterweight and picked two bricks off and threw them on the ground. The pulleys cracked against the captain's joints and he let out a pain-filled scream.

"Stop, I will kill you!" John yelled as he started toward Gabriel, who raised his gun and pointed it at his forehead.

The captain gasped out, "No, John, this is what *he* wants! It's all being recorded!"

"Go ahead, Corbin. Do it," Gabriel said as he knocked off another brick.

A grotesque popping sound came from the captain's right shoulder as bone, tendon, and flesh let go, followed by another scream.

"You son of a bitch!" John shouted.

Another brick was released, and his left shoulder was separated as well as his left knee. Another brick hit the ground and three of four limbs were detached, connected only by ragged flesh and skin. Captain Johnson's screams stopped as his head went limp. John watched in horror as Gabriel swiftly took a hunting knife that was strapped to his leg and sliced the rope, freeing the counterweight. The last of the bricks hit the ground and Captain Johnson's body was ripped apart, each limb propelled in a different direction. Blood poured from every unnatural orifice.

John was on him with his hands around his throat, squeezing as hard as he could, just like he had done to his brother Silas. John could feel the life draining out of Gabriel Crimson's body as a sinister smile appeared on the killer's lips. Suddenly, John thought of his children, his wife, and Ricky. He thought of learning from our past transgressions and redeeming ourselves when granted the opportunity. He thought of the captain and what he said before dying: "No, John! This is what he wants!"

John released Gabriel's throat, and slowly the life returned to his eyes as he gasped for breath. John grabbed the knife and cut a piece of rope from what remained. He turned the murderer over and tied his arms behind his back.

"Corbin, what are you doing? No..."

"Gabriel Crimson, you have the right to remain silent. Anything you say can and will be used against you in a court of law. You have the right to talk to a lawyer and have him present while you are being questioned."

"*NO! what are you doing you coward? Kill me!*"

"If you cannot afford a lawyer, one will be appointed to you. You can decide at any time to exercise these rights. Do you understand each of these rights I have explained to you?"

John tied Gabriel to a tree, sat, and glanced at what remained of his captain, his friend. He put his face in his hands and wept, not stopping until the spotlight from the helicopter fell on the scene.

CHAPTER NINE

There was no area for the copter to land, so Agent Phillips climbed the rope ladder down to the crime scene, handcuffed Crimson, and took him into custody. They called the local police to come and pick him up. Phillips stayed, monitored Crimson and waited for the arrival of the caravan of local cops, detectives, crime scene investigators, and press who were sure to follow. John shook hands with Phillips, thanked him, and climbed the ladder for the ride back to Seattle in the copter. He rested his head against the window and didn't move the whole journey back. He kept replaying the course of events over in his mind until, filled with exhaustion, mental trauma, and the lingering effects of a concussion, he drifted off to sleep.

John was woken with a thud as the helicopter landed. He was then transported from the air support unit to the station by vehicle. John walked in and headed for Daniels' office for debriefing and paperwork. He walked in on Daniels laying into Ricky. They each glanced up at John, but Daniels continued his onslaught.

"I told you no more BS, did I not? You kept all this from me. You communicate to a pedestrian, and he goes on a rogue mission himself to save Johnson? No wonder he's dead. You both failed to follow protocol, failed to do your jobs correctly, and now a good man is gone. Well, what do both of you have to say for yourselves?"

"Sir, I was instructed by the killer not to alert anyone of the situation or he would kill Michael."

"He killed him anyway!" Daniel yelled in Ricky's face. "Burton, I am advising this force to send you on unpaid leave for a month and let me tell you, if I advise it, it will happen."

"As you wish, sir," Ricky replied.

John noticed Daniels' eyes turn to him and he saw a spark in them. He was enjoying this. This piece of shit reveled in denigrating men that gave their heart and soul in an effort to save people.

"Well, Corbin? Who the fuck do you think you are, Johnny Rambo?"

John looked at Daniels, walked over and punched him square and hard on the chin. The malicious expression in his eyes was instantly replaced with shock as his chair collapsed and his body landed in a heap behind his pretentious, oversized desk. John turned to Ricky, gave him a quick hug, shook his hand, and walked out.

John entered his house without knowing what was waiting for him. Julie's car was in the driveway, which meant she didn't leave. The house was quiet aside from Simba running up to him like he hadn't seen him in ten years. Dogs have a way of always making a person feel wanted. It's no wonder why humans have grown to love them as not just pets, but members of the family. He walked upstairs and into the bedroom where Julie was out cold on the bed. On her nightstand was a bottle of sleeping pills which was unusual for Julie. She didn't approve of pills as a rule, and hardly ever gave any to their children.

"Julie, babe, wake up," he said as he slid into bed beside her and put his arms around her.

"John? You're here... alive!"

"Yes, I'm alive. Where are the children?"

"My Mother's, I needed to sleep. John, what happened?"

John looked away with his head down.

Julie sat up. "Is he... gone?"

"Yes. I tried Julie. He's dead."

Julie hugged him tight as she started to cry on his chest. "Does Sarah know?"

"Ricky has the unpleasant job of going to her house. I'm going to stop by there and talk to her tomorrow."

"I think that's a good idea. I didn't like your decision, but I understand it now. Are you okay?"

"Michael was like a father to me. He saved my life more than once. Watching him die ripped me apart inside, but that pain only goes so deep. We learn to keep a part of ourselves, a core, unavailable to anyone, or anything. That defense is instilled in us from the beginning. As soon as we witness that first bullet soar past our partner's head, or the first time we view a child's broken body from the stronghold of their abusive parents, or the first time we observe the dead bodies of innocent souls who had their lives taken because they were in the wrong place at the wrong time. Sensitivities become stunted, all in an attempt to preserve our sanities. I have successfully done that. Julie, I made that part of me, the innocence behind those walls, available to you, and now the children," John said, pausing for a moment to regain his focus. "I had to try to save him. It's what I am, but I am also sorry to put you through this."

Julie hugged him. "John, my love, don't apologize, I understand. And as much as I wanted to keep you from going, I knew you would. That's why I fell in love with you. What about the killer?"

"I got him. He is in custody."

John kissed his wife with a passionate hunger fueled by love. Love that we sometimes take for granted but are made aware of when we least expect it, when tragedy becomes possible. They made love with an urgency they hadn't felt in years.

THE REDEMPTION

***

The following two days, John stayed home with Julie and away from everyone. He needed to mourn, rest, and rekindle his drive to live. Dealing with the evil in the world for so long had impacted his ability to rebound as quickly as he used to and losing one of his best friends made it that much more difficult. He finally rolled out of bed late one morning and pushed himself to visit Sarah Johnson. After the short ride, he parked, walked to the door and knocked. Moments later the door swung open.

"John, hi, so nice to see you," she said as she gave him a hug.

"Sarah, I'm so sorry."

"Come in, John."

As he walked in and followed her to the sofa in the next room, he sensed something was off. He assumed she would have been nearly broken by the death of her husband, but she seemed settled, almost content.

"The funeral is tomorrow at Sacred Heart, at eleven."

"Okay, I will be there with my family. Sarah, are you okay?"

"I'm doing as well as expected, I guess."

"I tried, I did everything I could do—"

Sarah put her hand up to stop John mid-speech. "I know you did, and so does Michael. John, I am at peace. Michael came to me in my sleep. He told me everything will be fine, that we will be reunited when it's my time to leave this earth."

John searched her eyes for a sign of chaos, if the emotional turmoil had caused her to lose her hold on reality.

She smiled and said, "John don't look at me like that, you know I'm a very stable, sensible woman. He came to me; I know it was real."

John nodded and took her hand in his. "Is there anything I can do? Is there anything you need?"

"Just remember him. He loved you like a brother."

John dropped his head and surprisingly, he was the one crying.

They shared a cup of coffee together and toasted to Michael Johnson, the captain, friend, husband, and man he was throughout his life. It was time to go, and Sarah walked him to the door, hugged him again, and said goodbye. As John started down the walk to his truck, she called after him.

"I almost forgot, he wanted me to tell you something."

John stopped, turned, and awaited her secret.

"He said he is proud of you for letting go."

"What?"

Sarah shrugged. "Letting go of someone's throat. Also, he thanks you for Daniels… he never liked him."

Over a thousand people were present to pay their respects as Michael Johnson was laid to rest. The military gave a twenty-one-gun salute, thanking Michael for his service in the Gulf War. After the ceremonies, John stood by himself overlooking Captain Johnson's grave when Ricky walked up next to him and stood quietly. After a few moments, he broke the silence.

"Is this all there is?" Ricky asked quietly. "We end up here, earth and stone… we all go back to nature?"

"There is no secret to life. It seems we all search for that magical elixir, that hidden meaning that the others who have lived before us missed that will make us immortal, at least spiritually, if not physically. Truth is, there is no magical finish line any of us will cross victoriously. We live, we die, and the world goes on until everyone we have ever known joins us and generations spin on and on and on."

The two partners, friends, stood overlooking the grave until all others had left. Finally, the pair turned and walked away together.

The first call came at nine in the morning. John let it go to voicemail. In the proceeding days, a flood of calls followed, all looking for the same thing: an interview with the rapidly-becoming-famous hero, John Corbin. Every television station, radio station, and blog host within a twenty-five-mile radius wanted to nail John down for a time slot on their shows. John ducked them all. By the end of the afternoon, he had received over seventy-five messages. It was a full week since the incident in the Olympic forest, and John was planning on getting back to his restaurant full-time. Finally, a call came in from a number he recognized.

"Hello," John answered.

"Well, how does it feel to be famous, partner?"

"Hi Ricky, I wouldn't call it famous because my phone is blowing up with propositions from a bunch of parasites."

"Oh, it's more than that, KIRO-TV just aired a special on your story. They said, and I quote: "The bravery it took for Detective Corbin to offer himself up as bait in an attempt to save Captain Michael Johnson was legendarily heroic."

John grimaced. "Wonderful. I just want to be left alone, I'm no hero."

"Tell that to the masses, my friend. Hey, I miss ya, how about a drink tonight at the tavern?"

"Sure, I have to go over some scheduling issues with Red anyway. Eight o'clock work?"

"You got it, Dirty Harry."

"I'll see you then."

Just as John put his phone in his pocket there was a knock on the door. Assuming it was the press, he walked over preparing his negative response to whatever they wanted him to do. He tugged the door open while putting on a stern, assertive face. Standing on his doorstep were three handsome men who all looked to be in their fifties, dressed in suits.

"John Corbin?"

"I am. Gentlemen, if this is about a media spot, I'm really not interested."

"No, John, we aren't from the press," the leader said with an amused look on his face. "We're from the city council. I am City Manager, Barry Redding, and these are valued members of the council, James Moore, and Chris Tate. May we have a bit of your time?"

"Sure, come in," John replied.

The four men walked into the dining room and sat around the table.

"So, what's this about, Barry?"

"You've been approved as the predecessor of Captain Michael Johnson. Now, I know this will come as a shock and you've recently retired from the force, but we would very much like you to consider our offer."

John put his head back and ran his fingers through his hair.

"Now, please do not make a decision now," Barry Redding said quickly. "Take some time to think about it and talk to your family. If you decide to accept, we'll have a formal meeting to go over salary and benefits." Barry stood and the other gentlemen followed suit. "It would be an honor to have you serve as captain," Janes said. John followed them to the door to see them out.

"How long do I have to decide?"

"Take as long as you need."

"Thank you, gentlemen. Have a good day."

John watched them drive away with a slew of thoughts racing through his head.

John walked into an incredible scene. Everyone in the place gave him a standing ovation as he made his way to the bar where Ricky and Red awaited him.

"How does it feel to be famous?" Ricky asked as he sat down next to him. John noticed their three most loyal bar customers were even standing and clapping at the other end of the bar.

After the applause died down, John answered Ricky's question. "It doesn't feel like anything. Michael is dead. I'm no hero... I failed and lost a lifelong friend."

"We both did. I hadn't known him nearly as long as you, but I couldn't have respected the man more in the time we did have together."

"That's part of the deal. There is death around us all the time, and sometimes it really hits home. We give up the ability to smile as children do once we sign on."

"Smile as children?" Red said.

"Yes, smile freely without reservation, before we learned no form of love is unconditional and the human race is selfish and evil most of the time, before innocence was trampled and destroyed, never to return."

"Speaking of evil, did you know that Daniels pushed to press assault and battery charges against you? The brass vetoed him and told him to shut his mouth. They probably even gave him a bonus to keep quiet. They also reduced my suspension to two weeks paid."

"I was assuming something would come of that. Why did they veto it?"

Alan, a new bartender, placed shot-glass after shot-glass on the bar in front of him.

"Fuck's that?" John asked.

"All the free drinks you have waiting. The whole place is buying for you tonight."

Ricky continued: "They wanted a feel-good story with a hero. You'd be a difficult hero to sell to the press and public if they knew you walked in and slugged your superior officer."

"Yeah, well, fuck him."

Ricky burst out in laughter, as John and Red followed suit. When the amusement settled John became more serious.

"Listen, guys, I have something to tell you that may impact you both."

Ricky's face became stoic and Red turned and waited to hear John's secret.

"They offered me Michael's job."

"Captain? Of headquarters?"

"Yes."

"What did you tell them?" Red asked.

"I said I wanted to think about it. I wanted to talk to you guys and Julie before I make a decision."

"Well, I'm all for it, partner," Ricky said immediately and turned to look at Red.

"John, I know what your work means to you. You base your decision totally on that. We'll figure this place out if we have to. I'm doing fine, and we could hire a floor manager to help out if need be."

"Thanks, guys."

John ordered a round for the bar from his collection of free drinks. When Alan returned, he informed the bartender to give what was left to Sean, Artie, and Matt. John watched as the expression on Sean's face resembled a child on Christmas morning. He raised a glass in salute to his patrons.

The calls kept coming along with a constant stream of visitors from the press knocking on the door, which John had ceased to answer. Finally, John made a call to a friend who worked as a travel agent and was able to book a week-long cruise for four leaving Seattle the following day. Julie's parents agreed to stay in the house for a week to watch Simba. John, Julie, and the children said their goodbyes and headed for the Port of Seattle. They boarded the ship and just like that, were off on a week-long vacation, touring the coast of Northwest America, Canada, and Alaska.

On the third day of the cruise, the ship was docked in the Port of Juneau, Alaska, for a twelve-hour visit. They observed Mendenhall, an immense, twelve-mile-long river of ice, then tried out a scenic ziplining course, and finally settled in for a seafood dinner at a famous local restaurant.

"Dad, this is so awesome. I can't believe you just decided to take us on a cruise!" Ryann said excitedly.

"I really can't either. Sometimes you just have to set caution to the wind and go on an adventure," John replied as he gave Julie a warm smile.

"Dad, did you see that girl I was talking to on the glacier tour? She lives in Tacoma. She told me to look her up on Facebook," Ryann said as Gianna rolled her eyes.

"Wait, when the heck did that happen?" John turned to Julie for an explanation.

"It happened on the tour..."

"Not that particular girl, Ryann. When did you become interested in girls in general?"

"Since his friends decided too," Gianna interjected.

"You two need to slow down a bit. Stop growing up so fast, you'll regret it in ten years."

"Dad, we can't control how fast we grow."

"He didn't mean it literally, you dork," Gianna said.

"Oh. I can't believe I got a girlfriend, all the way up here!"

"Life is strange, son. You never know the really important moments are important when they're happening until you look back realizing the differences they made. I met your mother one night long ago because I promised a ten-year-old girl who was shot that she would be okay. Tabatha Jones, I'll never forget that name. Anyway, your mother was working at the hospital that night. That's when we met."

"Did she live?" Gianna asked.

"Yes, she did. Needless to say, I had a very good night," John answered. "So, I guess my point is every moment, no matter how seemingly insignificant, must be navigated with extreme thought. We never know when a major point in our lives is upon us."

John woke at the break of dawn on the last day of the cruise. He stepped out onto the upper deck, which had become his custom in the early morning before the rest of his family woke. It had been a wonderful vacation. They visited Skagway, Glacier Bay, Ketchikan, and Victoria, as well as Juneau. It was a perfect morning, warm, but not humid at all, with a crisp breeze coming from the west. He climbed to the top deck and walked to the end, put his hands on the rail and absorbed the beauty. He took in the blue-green ocean before turning his attention to the sky. He noticed the clouds, which are nothing but shaped air and condensation but also, ironically, the source of life. They moved rapidly across his vision and he thought about how they resemble the people in our lives, coming and going in the blink of an eye. They appear and vanish every day, looking down at us from the heavens, reminding us of our own immortality. His thoughts turned to Todd and his family, Captain Johnson, and all the others that were lost through the years.

But life is for the living, and John wasn't finished living yet.

He took one last look across the horizon, turned and started his walk back. This was the last day for this vacation and he was going to make the best of it because memories are all we have long after our lives end.

THE END

About the Author

David Boiani is a dedicated father to a wonderful eighteen-year-old daughter in her first year of college, member of The Association of Rhode Island Authors, and guitarist in an originals alternative rock band called The Whole façade.

David's love of reading ignited his desire to write fiction. The Redemption, sequel to A Thin Line, is his third book.

For more information and to purchase his books, see special promotions, and sign up for his newsletter, please visit:

http://www.authordavidboiani.com/

Also by This Author:

DARK MUSINGS

What if real life scenarios were far more horrific than fantasy? What if you could visit the dark, unsettling mind of one man and experience the disturbing stories that originate there?

These stories are unconnected, but they all include a similar trait: Fear. They are all based on aspects of life that are haunting yet very real. Experiencing these stories will induce a terror that will stay with you long after the final page is turned...

THE REVIEWS ARE IN!

"Haunting, frightening, yet beautiful and bringing up important truths about us, human beings."

"These are tales that might happen, some that do happen. It is not a journey for the faint of heart. However, I also feel it is one that most should read."

"Haunting, intriguing, some of them downright frightening, but at the end of the day, for me, they were ultimately uplifting, giving a sense of something greater than ourselves at work."

"This collection of short stories will make you think about life, death, love, family, spirituality, and the human condition. The thoughts within can be dark at times, as the title suggests, but even in the darkness there is always some hope, no matter how small."

A THIN LINE

What if a man lost his moral compass between right and wrong, good and evil, mental stability and insanity?

John Corbin has been investigating, catching, and convicting murderers, rapists, and pedophiles for twenty years as a Seattle detective. But lately, someone has been beating him to the punch and eliminating these vile criminals before he can apprehend them. John is learning that there is a thin line between innocent or guilty, good or evil, alive or dead.

By definition, a thin line is a very narrow division between two alternatives. Some being exact opposites, while others are separated by the narrowest of threads. This novel follows this definition to the letter. In life, many situations aren't just black or white. There is usually a modicum of grey to fill in the space. Who is right? Who is wrong? Who is good? Who is evil? Perhaps everyone at one time or another lies somewhere in the middle....

A Thin Line is a tale that will immediately draw you in and keep you guessing. A suspenseful psychological thriller with twists and turns that will toy with your mind and emotions, driven by a chilling narrative that builds the tension right up until its explosive conclusion.

THE REVIEWS ARE IN!

"This is the raw, horrible, gruesome, human-as-a-horror truth of man's depravity."

"You will read this book and in certain chapters, it will be so disturbing that you will wonder what is wrong with the guy writing this book, why is this book so DARK. Then you will stop and realize that crimes like this happen every single day. The author just finds a way of forcing you to deal with them."

"The ending was more than surprising, and I applaud the author since I never saw that coming. The characters were very well developed and the storyline gritty and fast-paced. Great work."

"I'm still reeling from this book! It's a really good, gritty read that caught me by surprise. This was my first time reading this author, and wow - I was blown away."

Other Titles Available from Foundations Book Publishing Company

EVIN
By A.S. Crowder

Eva has never seen the Forest of Evin, but her fate and the fate of the Forest may be intertwined.

Sinister forces seek to pull the Forest apart, and Eva may be the only one who can save it. Eva must travel between worlds to keep the Forest together...

...but the Forest of Evin thrums with power and the force tearing it apart may not be the only danger.

Dark Prisoner – The Kruthos Key
By D. Thomas Jerlo

Suna Di'Viao, the last of the Divenean race, has hidden from the world, blaming herself for the demise of King Markes and Queen Saliste.

It's a fate she believes she deserves, but when she's summoned on a quest by a mysterious stranger, her Divenean heritage won't allow her to refuse.